SPACE DRAGONS

ROBIN BENNETT

BOOKS

Space Dragons (Monster Books Ltd)

Published in Great Britain by
Monster Books
The Old Smithy
Henley-on-Thames
Oxon. RG9 2AR

First published 2018; this new paperback edition published in 2020.

ISBN 9781916375130

A catalogue record of this book is available from the British Library.

Printed by Clays Ltd., Bungay, Suffolk.

To little sisters across the known universe.

And beyond.

CHAPTER 1

The whole universe:
every planet, star, black hole and life form
started with a single atom
exploding into a great void of nothing.

Right after that, came the Dragons.

IF STAN POLLUX had known he would be spending the rest of his summer holidays in the outer reaches of our solar system, he would have put on different underpants.

The ones he wore the morning when it all began were too tight and had a faded picture of Ben Ten on the back, which made them look like the child superhero had been specially assigned by the Pants People to guard his butt.

Right now, however, he had more important

things on his mind. He looked at the pieces of his broken telescope and thought angrily about his little sister.

'You're so stupid! You broke it and even after you were told not to go in my room, or touch my stuff!' he'd shouted. She was the one who had smashed his telescope but he was the one who got into trouble for making her cry, when it wasn't her fault, according to their mother – although of course it was! She'd knocked the telescope over. It was obviously *all* her fault.

It was also pretty annoying that Stan hadn't been given any time to sort out the mess until the evening. First it was lunch, then he'd been made to clean up the early fallen apples at the bottom of the garden. Once in a while, he had looked up from what he'd been doing to see Poppy peering at him from behind the bushes. He'd scowl and she'd dart off.

Stan knew she was sorry, and what's more he knew she hadn't meant to smash the telescope.

'It's really not nice to be horrible to your little sister all the time, she adores you.' His mother had said. A small, guilty part of him knew that, too. 'You used to play so well together.' And that.

Then they'd been taken food shopping in town, which was almost worse than doing chores and it

wasn't until after supper that Stan was allowed to go upstairs and check out the damage properly.

Stan lived with his parents (Mr and Mrs Pollux), his sister, Poppy (short for Penelope – or, Small Annoying Person), and their dog, Boris. They lived in a really old and, therefore, slightly falling down house on the edge of the village. His dad had told him the kitchen and two of the bedrooms upstairs dated from the Middle Ages, when the village had been famous for having a witch who had been hanged. Some people even said that the witch had grown up in their house: Guy Murphy, the school bully, had given Stan nightmares in Year 5 by telling him her ghost crept about in the woods close by at night, looking for a way into their house. To get revenge.

As he climbed the back stairs, Stan remembered the story and shivered. He was in Year 7 now, but he still avoided looking out of his bedroom window, at the dark trees crowding the end of their garden, like waiting figures in ragged shrouds.

When he got into his room it was ablaze in a blood-red glow from the setting Sun. He got into his pyjamas, watching as the skies darkened at the top of the window frame and one or two stars winked into view: tiny silver dots millions and mil-

lions of miles away.

Stan shivered once more, in spite of the summer evening, closed the curtains quickly and turned on the electric light. It was one of those nights when everything felt weird and a bit spooky.

❄

By the time Stan had got his telescope back on its stand, properly screwed in, and had checked it carefully for dents, the sunset had receded to a fiery fringe on the horizon and the skies were as bottomless and black as infinity itself.

He was so wrapped up in inspecting his telescope, that he didn't notice the open display box on the floor which housed his crystal collection. If he had, he would have seen that there was a gap in the neat rows of polished stones, meaning one was missing. The missing crystal was one given to him by his grandmother. It was his largest piece and, strangest of all, warm to the touch – even on a really cold day. Stan had tried looking it up online but nothing on any of the collectors' sites seemed to match the orange glow that came from within its core. He'd asked his granny where she'd got it from, but she had looked shifty, and dismissed his questions with

a wave of her bony hand. Anyway, if Stan had glanced down he would have seen it was gone. But he didn't.

This is important.

Instead, Stan opened the curtains again and peered at the skies. For as long as he could remember, Stan was fascinated with anything to do with Space.

'So what is it you like so much about other planets and solar systems?' His teacher, Miss Quinn, had asked him more than once. Questions like this from adults always made Stan deeply uncomfortable. In his experience adults always wanted the right answer to questions and this was one of those where a right answer was impossible. Usually you could sort of guess what an adult needed to know. For example: Did you brush your teeth? Answer: Yes (whether you had or not); Did you hit your sister? Answer: No, she just fell over. There were rules to yes/no questions. Stan knew where you were with rules and he liked to stick to them. But this one was harder. And pointless because no one was saying anything useful: it was just chatting.

'Well ...?' Miss Quinn could be impatient.

'Dunno,' he had mumbled. He wished adults – teachers and parents, in particular – could give

more clues when they asked things. If Miss Quinn had said, *Do you like Space because it's this great big mystery, like a huge open door that could lead anywhere and we've only just peeked in*, then he could have said *yes* and then he could go and get on with other things. Other things than talking.

And Space was a mystery. More than that. Space was *unfathomable*. Stan had read that in a magazine and he liked the word. It had interesting syllables and it was good for describing depth: as if Space was like a huge deep sea with no bottom, and spacecraft were more like powerful submarines than ships. It was all out there for the looking and imagining: aliens, fireballs, black holes, wormholes and supernovas ...

The telescope had been his mother's idea, who just loved the thought of anything educational, but Stan had gone for it immediately. It had cost so much it had been a combined birthday and Christmas present and, even then, Mum and Dad put some extra money in so he could get the one all the websites raved about. It was called a Vision4000 and it could magnify objects 180 times, so the Moon basically looked 180 times bigger than when you looked at it normally.

Just about anything, 180 times bigger, was going

to look pretty cool.

Stan took hold of the eyepiece.

As he was setting it back up, the scope had seemed fine, no dents on the shiny black tube and the stand wasn't bent from where Poppy had knocked it over when she had gone into his room. However, as he moved it, he felt something rattle in the cylinder. He gave the scope a gentle shake and it rattled again, like a loose screw was inside.

Stan's palms were sweaty as he handled the cool tube and it was then that he finally admitted to himself that he felt nervous. But was it just the telescope? Everything felt creepy tonight. He took a deep breath, removed the lens cap and peered down the eyepiece.

Nothing. And, yet, there was something about the deep blackness at first glance that didn't look like right: it almost felt as if he was staring into a hole in Space, and as if, from the end of this long, dark tunnel, something was hiding. And waiting.

Stan shook his head. He was just imagining things. He glanced up ... nope, the Moon was bright in the sky between two large oaks at the end of the garden. Stan checked he was pointing it in the right direction for him to see its reassuring silvery light and looked again.

Nothing. Just a deep, flat blackness. OK, so his telescope was broken! Stan felt his fear driven away by anger. Resisting the urge to rush downstairs yelling, or straight into his sister's room, Stan swung the scope around ...

An evil-looking eye, from the depths of Space, sprang open and stared back.

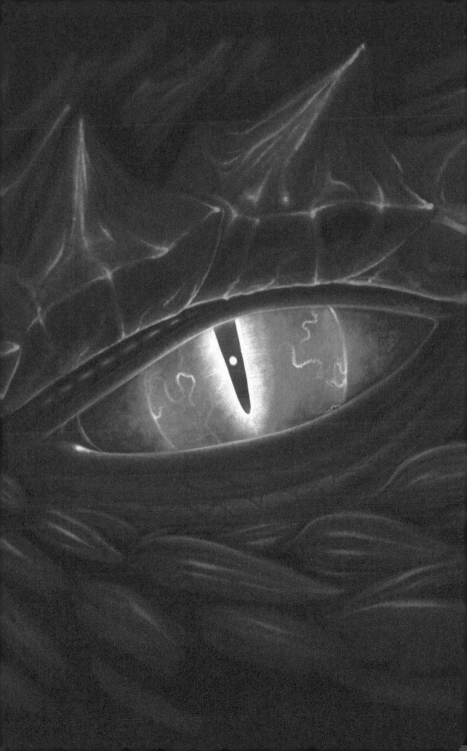

CHAPTER 11

Space thinks big: the Sun, our nearest star,
is 11,000 times larger than the Earth.
Canis Majoris, a star in a system near ours,
is 1,200 times larger than our Sun.

❄

THE NEXT MORNING Stan came downstairs looking peaky.

'Morning Stan,' his mother said, all muffly. She had an armful of laundry covering most of her face, and a piece of toast in her mouth.

Stan nodded vaguely, stepped around her and sat down at the breakfast bar. He didn't much feel like talking, he had rather a lot on his mind. He stared at the local paper lying on the counter without really seeing it, then poured a bowl of cereal into a bowl and started to eat.

The eye.

Vast: orange and gold swirling flames within. Stan had a horrible feeling it wasn't just the telescope

11

that made it look so huge.

Poppy came downstairs, a jumper over her nightie, and looked at her brother. 'You've forgotten to put any milk on your cornflakes,' she pointed out solemnly. 'Mummy, Stan's eating cereal without milk!'

'Good,' said their mother, who was now going the other way through the kitchen carrying an assortment of jumpers, homework books, trainers, sweet wrappers and toys to distribute around other parts of the house. 'We'll save a fortune.'

'But —' Poppy stopped. Stan was staring at her. He looked a bit mad.

'What did you do to my telescope?' His voice was low and their mother was the other side of the house fussing with the curtains in the living room. Poppy's bottom lip quivered. She had been hoping Stan had forgotten all about yesterday.

'Nothing, it was just an accident —'

'I saw ... an *eye*,' Stan continued spooning dry cornflakes into his mouth and staring at nothing.

'Well,' replied Poppy, who clearly thought it was high time to look on the bright side of the whole incident, 'that means it's working.'

Stan just sat there, dry cornflakes clogging his mouth. He was playing over what had happened:

The Eye.

Penetrating: surrounded by blackness it had blinked once, then swivelled in his direction and Stan had felt the heat of its gaze burning into him. Right through him, in fact.

He had the distinct impression that in one glance that eye, or the owner of it, knew more about Stan than anyone alive. Most importantly – and, at this point, the cereal suddenly tasted like cold ashes – the owner of The Eye knew exactly where he lived.

The instant he'd seen it staring back at him, Stan had panicked and had fallen backwards onto his bed. Then, on reflection, he had grabbed a pillow and covered his face, closing his own eyes tight, concentrating on his breathing and the sound of his heart thumping in his chest, half expecting something terrible to smash through the window at any moment.

He had stayed like that for a very, very long time.

Eventually, as dawn turned the room from black to wolf grey, he had crawled beneath the sheets and slipped into strange dreams.

'Whose shoes are these? Bad dog!' His mother, scolding Boris downstairs, had woken him. So, he had got up, still in his clothes from the previous day, and had gone downstairs: carefully avoiding

looking at his telescope as he went past.

'It is broken,' Stan looked up from his dry cereal and glared at his sister, relieved that the anger seemed to be taking his mind off his fear from the long night. 'And it's all your fault, you'll have to pay me back with all your pocket money and you'll probably have to sell your stupid Bunny and your even stupider doll collection.'

Poppy went pink and looked on the verge of tears again. 'But I said I was sorry. Daddy can fix it.'

'Mum?' Stan turned to his mother who seemed to be looking for something.

'What is it, darling?'

'The telescope's broken and —'

'OK, I'll get your father to look at it when he gets back from Brussels.'

'But—Poppy ...' Stan had no idea where he was going with this, just that he thought his sister was getting away with it. As usual.

Poppy, who had not had positive and immediate confirmation that her Bunny wasn't going to end up on eBay had started to cry. Their mother gave up looking for where she'd left her tea and turned to them both.

'Poppy said she was sorry. She shouldn't have been in your room but if you were nicer to her about

sharing, she wouldn't have panicked and knocked your telescope over when she heard you coming. Poppy, stop blubbing, no one's going to take your toys – lovely though he is, I doubt we'd even be able to give Bunny away on eBay ... but you've been told not to go into Stan's room, so don't.' Poppy sniffed very loudly.

'Yes Mummy.'

'Now, you've both got six weeks' holiday and you're going to have to get on, or you'll be doing chores and homework for most of it.' Their mother turned and marched out of the room with purpose: her tea was by the front door on the telephone table.

❄

The day was bright and hot, with a sky so blue it almost seemed black. It was the sort of summer's day that you only get once or twice a year in England. Stan had stayed in the garden since breakfast, carefully avoiding his room and Poppy. He and Dad had started building a treehouse at the far end by the compost, and he took his mind off things by trying to nail walls to the platform they had already built together.

His dad was a photographer who specialised in taking pictures of politicians and people on the sort of programmes Stan turned off because there was just talking, which was the last thing Stan was into. His dad's job meant that he was away a lot, travelling to where the politicians were having their next talking match, but when he did come back it was usually for a couple of weeks and lots got done and his mother seemed less stressed. The treehouse was coming along pretty well and, if he was able to get the walls up in the next week or so, they'd be able to finish it together over a weekend.

Stan had a lot of free weekends, these days: things weren't that good at school. And that was Poppy's fault, too.

All that summer term, he'd been avoiding his friends – although Stan had a feeling they'd been avoiding him back. Since the incident at the bus stop with Poppy, there had been at least three birthday parties. He'd waited for his invitation as they'd been handed out by his classmates before assembly, then had to pretend he hadn't noticed when the last one had gone and there was no envelope with his name on it.

In spite of promising himself he wouldn't, Stan now played the Incident at the Bus Stop back in his

head for about the millionth time.

*

'You mustn't hurt Stan, he's my big brother and that's not very nice!' Poppy stood in front of his classmates who were smirking at Stan's little sister who had gone red in the face, hands on hips, her frizzy, blond hair was sticking out in all directions. Stan felt his own cheeks burning and his eyes pricked with the start of tears, more in shame than the pain in his arm where Guy Murphy had shown everyone his new judo hold on him. Everyone had laughed, especially when Guy used it to nick Stan's crisps. He started to munch on them noisily, his hands covered in flecks of salt and crumbs.

'What are you going to do about it, Stan's little sister, whose name I can't be bothered to remember?' Guy was enjoying himself as he sensed the crowd of kids at the bus stop were on his side.

... It's not what she's going to do about it, it's me you should be worried about, Murphy ...

That's what Stan should have said, or something like that. But, as usual, what was in his head and what came out were two very different things. Most of the time, he only thought of something to say

17

long afterwards.

'Yeah, what's that?' Guy had turned his attention back to Stan. 'Mumbling again? Come on spit it out, Stammering Stan, as usual no one can hear you. I tell you what,' Guy grinned nastily, 'if you can say ... *supercalifragilisticexpialidocious* really fast or ... ah ... *she sells sea shells on the seashore*, I'll give your crisps back.' More giggles and flecks of crisps hit Stan in the face.

The dumb thing was, he was much bigger than Guy Murphy, but the smaller boy had always found a way to make Stan feel stupid. All the fight in him would just trickle away, like now, so he felt slow and brainless and didn't know whether to laugh along with the joke against him or finally shut Guy Murphy up once and for all. Stan opened his mouth and closed it – like a big, stupid fish – and, all the time he stood there doing nothing, he could see Poppy out of the corner of his eye looking up at him expectantly.

'Um ... come on ... please Guy,' he had eventually mumbled, 'can I have my crisps back?'

'Stan!' Poppy was completely outraged.

'I'm bored of this!" Guy suddenly announced. He pushed Stan roughly in the chest, 'get away from me anyway, you stink bad!'

'You don't say that, you give his crisps back!'

'Forget it Poppy, let's just go home,' Stan mumbled again, half turning to walk away.

'Yeah, that's right, jog on Pollux and next time you get your little sister to fight your battles, you tell her she's going upside down in that bin.'

... Lay a finger on her and you'll be lucky to get your arm back, Murphy ...

... but that never came out, either: he had grabbed Poppy by the elbow and pulled her away.

'But Stan ...' she turned and glared at Guy who was laughing his head off.

'Shut up, Poppy, just walk!'

'B—' she saw the look on his face. 'OK, but I'm telling Mummy, when we get home.'

'No, you're not!'

'Alright, Stan.'

❄

At this point Stan came out of his day-nightmare and realised he was manically banging a nail into a plank that had long since disintegrated into splinters. He shook away the awful memory, and wondered if he would ever be able to think about his little sister trying to protect him as Guy Murphy ate

his crisps without wanting to crawl under his bed and stay there forever.

Stan swung out of the treehouse and moved to the paddling pool, lying full length fully clothed. He didn't care if he got into trouble for being soaking wet. Instead, he stared up at the friendly blue sky. Within a few minutes he had begun to relax for the first time since the night before ... he even began to feel sleepy ... perhaps he'd just imagined whatever he thought he saw through his telescope.

Yet where Stan now lay, feeling safe and warm again, he had not noticed that the grass had been flattened all around: squashed by something very large and very heavy. As it so happened, Stan was blissfully unaware that he was lying in the bowl of a paw print, topped with three huge claw marks.

And that he was still being watched.

❄

CHAPTER III

Are dinosaurs just another word for Dragons?

❄

IT'S AMAZING HOW MUCH BRAVER you feel after two helpings of spaghetti bolognese followed by chocolate mousse. Stan wolfed down his supper that night – he was in a hurry to get upstairs as soon as it got dark. In between mouthfuls, he would glance out of the window, hoping against clouds, but the sky remained clear as it went from blue to black in the space of half an hour.

Poppy was dawdling over her portion, looking at him with large eyes whilst he ignored her; and his mum seemed glued to her tablet. Stan grabbed an apple and took it upstairs.

'Put your dirty clothes outside your door, before they start to walk about by themselves,' Mrs Pollux said without looking up, 'and don't stay up too late, even if it is the holidays.'

'No Mum.'

'Goodnight Stan,' said Poppy hopefully, but he ignored her.

❄

As soon as he got into his room, he felt the same electrical charge in the air from the evening before, as if something big was about to happen. The Sun had slipped off the edge of the world, like a burning spacecraft sinking below the event horizon, and the stars were appearing randomly, like coded messages.

The telescope stood where he had left it, lens caps off, tube tilted upwards, more or less where Stan knew Venus, the nearest and brightest planet, would be visible. Most clear nights you could see it without a telescope.

He started to move the tripod and boxes around the end of his bed. This time he would set the telescope up closer to the window. This way there would be less light coming from the room, less chance of a reflection making him imagine seeing something ...

Stan stopped.

He stared hard at the gap in the display box where his rock and crystal collection was housed. He felt a

new wave of anger and clenched his fists very hard ... it had to be Poppy ... why she had been in his room was suddenly clear – she had been playing with the crystals, especially the one from Granny, which she loved ... then she heard him coming back and had panicked and knocked his telescope over.

But the crystal was gone.

At first, Stan was going to race into her room and demand it back, but she'd just deny it – as usual. Right now, he had something more important to do – however annoying it was, the crystal would have to wait until the morning.

He swung the telescope around, hearing that rattle again, but also noticing how the metal was warm, quite unlike the evening before. He ran his fingers along the smooth black casing, towards the end. It was almost too hot to touch.

Some of his fear from the night before was beginning to creep back: the dark corners in his room looked darker, the shaded trees outside seemed to be hiding things and the silence made him super aware of scratching sounds from the attic. He took a deep breath before it got any worse and forced himself to look through the viewfinder.

Nothing.

Stan panned across the sky to the sector where

there was a dusting of distant stars – the Milky Way. He looked again.

Nothing.

Stan sighed, yet, at the same time, he was somewhat relieved there were no huge eyes lost in space, glaring at him. Let's face it, he told himself, his telescope was useless now – one of the lenses must have become dislodged when it toppled over. He couldn't be bothered to feel angry now. He would just add it to the long list of things of his that Poppy had lost or broken. His dad would get it fixed ... but when?

Idly, he swung the telescope towards the Moon that had risen to just beyond the tops of the trees. The complicated and delicate lenses were definitely loose, because even the silver-grey brightness coming from the nearest body to the Earth didn't show up so much as a smudge. All Stan got was the reflection of his own pupil, jerking this way and that, and his lashes blinking back at him ...

Without warning, he saw a shape, like a huge black wing, flick across the telescope's point of focus. He looked again, it was gone.

Forgetting his fear, Stan swung the scope around in all directions, black, black, nothing, black, nothing ... then ... there! A pair of wings, ragged and

huge, arced and went out of focus. It was hard to move around in the cramped room and he could only see out one side of the house, so Stan shoved away the scope and looked out of the window with his own eyes. He could see nothing here, but what if he went outside?

His heart thumped in his chest, but more with excitement: he'd forgotten his previous sense of fear as he grabbed the telescope and ran down the back stairs. The whole point of being serious about having a telescope was to discover things. But what had he just seen?

His mother was watching TV with the living room door half closed, so it was easy to slip out.

Racing into the warm night air in the back garden, Stan set his scope up and looked. This time he was more methodical, searching one section of the night sky for a few moments, then moving on, turning slowly clockwise. He felt a fizz of excitement, sure he would spot the wing again at any moment. What was it? It looked like it could belong to a bat but Stan had focused the scope far beyond the flight of anything that flew. This was out there, beyond the Earth's atmosphere ... but that was impossible!

It was warmer than expected in the garden. In

fact, Stan felt positively hot, even more so than he had during the day. Sweat had begun to trickle down the back of his neck as he shifted the lens around another few inches. He went to wipe it off with his hand when he felt warm air ruffle the hair on the back of his head, then stop.

Then it came again.

Regular gusts that were getting stronger ... before he could turn around, a sound like a bellows went HUMPHRRR! and the air that had been pleasantly warm, suddenly felt unpleasantly hot as the hair on the nape of Stan's neck parted. Stan froze, looked away from the viewfinder and saw his shadow thrown out across the garden by a light coming from behind his back.

He turned ... ever so ... slowly.

A mass of silver scales, two black wings and two eyes like car lights.

Before Stan could embarrass himself by screaming, a plume of white hot flame shot up into the night sky, knocking the scope over, and Stan felt himself being wrenched up, as if caught in its stream, past the roof of their house and the tops of the trees, and with a sudden burst of unimaginable speed he burst through some wisps of cloud and into the upper atmosphere.

And, just like that, Stan Pollux was gone.

Back in the garden all was still again, as if nothing had happened with no one at all to witness it. All, that is, except for a small pair of bright eyes that watched from her bedroom window. Little fingers held onto the coloured crystal she'd taken the day before from Stan's room.

Poppy had no doubt in her young mind that this was somehow all her fault.

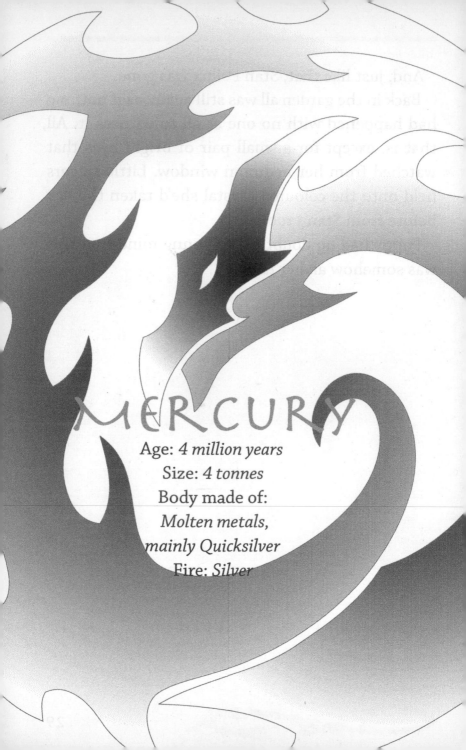

MERCURY

Age: *4 million years*
Size: *4 tonnes*
Body made of:
Molten metals,
mainly Quicksilver
Fire: *Silver*

CHAPTER IV

The Babylonians were the first people
to discover the planets
and to worship them as gods.

❋

FOR OVER TEN THOUSAND YEARS no Human had been enclosed in a Dragon's aura, so Stan could be forgiven for having absolutely nothing to compare it to except it was like being in a lift with no walls, that made no sound except for ... he listened carefully, a faint murmuring, like a church choir very far away.

Immediately it happened, he knew he was going up, because the light coming from the kitchen, and those of the other kitchens and living rooms in the village, then the outlines of the hills around, the familiar woods and fields, the orange glow of Oxford – in fact everything Stan knew and cared about – stretched far, far away in a matter of seconds. Soon nothing even slightly familiar or

comforting could be seen as the sky became darker and the curve of the Earth expanded like a giant beach ball.

Stan's first proper thought, other than *I will never, ever go into the garden at night again* was one of surprise that he was not freezing cold, or running out of oxygen or that his arms and legs hadn't been torn off with the force of the speed at which they were going. Instead, he felt light and ever so slightly sleepy in a sort of cosy, *well, I'll just sit here and watch the world go by kind of way*. Which was exactly what he was doing.

He thought he should be jumping up and down, crying out for help and generally panicking (let's face it, he was being kidnapped by a very big silver Dragon) so, with nothing better to do, he gave it a go.

'Agggggghhhhh help me I'm going to die, I can't breathe, I'm going to fallllllll, aaarghhhh, heeeeeellppp!!' and so on. In fact, Stan said more in the first few thousand miles of being inside the Dragon's aura than he'd said that whole year.

Except no one was listening.

He was now in Space, which he knew was one big vacuum: no air, no heat and, most importantly, no sound.

More to the point, he had a feeling that if he did manage to get so much as ten feet from this protective tunnel all around him, all of the terrible things he imagined, plus a couple of others he had only just thought of (exploding eyeballs) would definitely happen.

So, after ten minutes, his throat slightly sore, Stan decided to shut up, stay put and go back to enjoying the view.

And what a view it was! No satellite photo, CGI, VR or artist can really capture what it is to be looking out over the whole world. The Earth was now a lot smaller and, when he turned, he saw the Moon coming up on his left: huge and greyish white but very familiar. Everything was bright: the blue of the Earth's oceans was more blue than he would ever have imagined, the land masses greener and, from where he was, he could still see Britain and make out the rest of Europe and America. When he turned his head, looking out into Space, he gasped at the deep rich black panorama of velvet with the stars and planets scattered like cut diamonds: up, down, all around, everywhere and every which way he turned.

The murmuring chant he noticed before became louder and he realised it definitely was music: nice

relaxing melodies, like lullabies his mother sang when he was little. Stan yawned. He really did feel very sleepy ....

❄

Stan slept, and as he did so, he dreamt.

He was riding on the back of a huge Dragon whose rainbow scales: crimson, cobalt blue and bronze flashed in the reflective fire of some great battle far below as they burst through skyscrapers of flame. His legs, encased in golden armour, gripped the Dragon's flanks and he felt its great heart beat in time with its wings. Stan looked through the visor of his helmet and saw they were approaching a colossal sun. As the heat enveloped them, Stan felt storm winds buffet his polished breastplate and his chain mailed hands gripped tighter ... the Dragon flew directly towards the swirling skies and burning gases ... but something was wrong with this sun: when Stan looked at the surface he could see a dark spot, as if something was missing ... Stan stirred in his dream ... frowning. He could see what was wrong.

The Sun was dying.

❄

'Well, when Venus told me, I could have fallen off my big throne, if I'd been sitting down on it, not flying about, a swooshing and a somersaulting in the great firmament what is the heavens and all that ... By Bellona's beard! First Human to have clapped eyes on us in a thousand generations ... shouldn't be possible across two whole dimensions, but you ... you just looked through a loooong tube thingama-watucallit, Venus says, and BANG ... saw her plain as Saturn's rings. She was all for coming right down and eating you on the spot.'

Someone was talking.

Stan wasn't sure who they were talking to but, in case it was him (and an answer was expected), he kept his eyes closed tight.

'... soooo she shoots off to my place next door, *need someone reliable* she purrs, someone fast – well, never been able to say no to Venus – who has? ... those eyes ... she's still got it! Whatever *it* is ... pro-vided you're selective and the lighting's right ... if you know what I mean ... they always say the eyes are last to go but anyone who's met Medusa might beg to differ – and I know one or two Cyclops ... anyway, where was I? Oh, yes ... so I said *let's take a look first ... I'll go down, talk to this manchild who has*

35

seen us and tell you what it's all about ... it's my job after all! And she says yes, I've been studying the stars, the old enemy may be coming back and the Particle of Light is in play and so I say sounds serious, bye! and off I go, back to the Old Planet ... absolutely the wrong sun cycle for travel between dimensions ... but, I'm a martyr to my duties, anyway it's been a while and good to have an excuse to get out ...'

Stan was fairly sure they were no longer moving through the tunnel of fire. In fact they seemed to have stopped completely. He must have dropped off for a while. He wriggled his shoulders: he was lying down on something soft and very comfortable.

'... tellin' our lot what's what, who's up to this 'n' that, or just flying about their home planet minding their own business. Anyway, now you're here and I'm here – s'far as I can tell, though I'm a bit shaky these days on all this multidimensional stuff – we can have a nice long talk ... So ...?'

Stan, who usually felt like the last thing he wanted to do was have a conversation, even with people he knew quite well, kept his eyes shut and pretended to be still asleep. He felt warm – very warm – air blowing over him.

'You're not very *chatty*, are you?'

Stan sighed inwardly and opened his eyes.

They were in some sort of cave, except it wasn't dark – quite the opposite, in fact – and the walls, ceiling and floor didn't seem to be made of rock, but solid, shining silver. Stan squinted in awe at shimmering surfaces that hurt his eyes and the long, tapering stalactites, like swords, spearing pools of silvery liquid. Where was he? He sat up, noticing how he did not seem so much resting on the hard, metallic surface – rather floating above it on a force field that was springy, like a bouncy castle.

He scanned around the chamber, his mouth slowly falling open until his eyes got around to the voice.

Stan stared. Really stared.

The most remarkable thing was that the creature in front of Stan appeared to be made of molten metal: his scales flowed and rippled and everything about him shone deep, lead-silver. With his wings tucked away, his kidnapper wasn't as big as he remembered from the night before – about the size of a very large elephant, if Stan had to put it into context. The creature saw Stan staring and spread his wings and rose up on two strong legs.

'I'm Mercury, Messenger of the gods!' He boomed in an unexpectedly loud voice that made the pools

of liquid silver ripple, then he winked at Stan, as if winking was something he'd only read about in a book. 'Wotcha.'

Incredibly, given the circumstances, Stan remembered countless reminders from his mum. 'Er, I'm Stan, I hope you're fine.'

The silver dragon came closer and Stan felt some of his fear return. It peered at Stan, '... something has been bothering me since I nabbed you. 'Why do you smell of the Particle of Light?'

Stan had no idea what his captor was talking about but he felt he needed to add something else, 'I go to Long Wittenham Primary ... what's a Particle of Light?'

The Dragon smiled a toothy smile. 'Ooh good, you've got manners ... I like that in a Human, half the time they're whipping out a sword right now, banging on about smiting, calling us names like *foul beast* and *devil's spawn*, when half the time (speaking for myself, mind you) I'm only in this dimension for their own good, to tell them something important, and so what if I bite the head off a sheep or two? Hungry work, going about the cosmos informing ungrateful people about stuff. And, in case you are still wondering, we're on my planet, the Planet Mercury.' Mercury raised a

webbed wing, 'Ta! da!'

'Thank you very much,' said Stan carefully, not sure what he was being grateful about. He also noticed the Dragon had not answered his question. 'Can I go home now?' Yesterday the prospect of a long summer holidays with nothing planned seemed boring, now there was altogether far too much stuff going on in his life: most of which he didn't understand. The Dragon, who obviously thought some sort of sense of wonder and appreciation at being there was called for from Stan, looked a bit put out.

'Gods help us,' said Mercury, rolling his eyes, 'expected more of a sense of occasion.'

'Sorry,' said Stan, the last thing he wanted to do was get into an argument. 'Perhaps I can come back, a bit later?'

'Not so fast, there,' Mercury let out a small jet of silver flame. 'Fact is, we Dragons exist in another dimension, you shouldn't be able to see us. But *you*,' he prodded Stan with a claw, 'did. Venus is worried and I was sent to get some answers. First of which, how did you do that and secondly, the Particle of Light was something that shouldn't exist ... or it's been lost for so long ... yet, I remember that smell ...' Mercury seemed deep in thought, '... even after a

thousand generations. If the Particle is back, it means she's right, They are coming, and *that* means we're all in trouble, so I'll need to get the word out!'

Stan tried to focus, although it was hard with several tonnes of Dragon sniffing him. 'I don't know what a Particle of Light is.'

Mercury looked at him again. Very hard. 'Yet, you've been in contact with it, and recently too ... hmmm ... questions and no answers ... the others will say I haven't been doing my job.' Mercury continued to stare at him. Stan stared back, deciding he was going to say the minimum from now, until he knew what was going on.

'Anyway, my new young friend of the Fourth Dimension, your kind has not been able to summon a Dragon for many thousands of years – sorry if that was a bit of an ordeal, couldn't really think of any other way to get you off the planet – and we're back here in my Aura, safe and sound in the cosy Seventh Dimension, in case you were wondering.'

Stan suddenly felt he was on surer ground. 'Mr. Dobson says there's only four dimensions, all the rest are just made up.'

The Dragon gave a long whistle. 'Listen to you! So just where do you think you are now?'

'We can only exist in the Fourth Dimension,' said

Stan, who had been listening very carefully when the science teacher from the secondary school came to give them a special lesson about Space, 'the other ones don't have Time.'

'Well, you lot seem to have come on a bit since I was last back,' Mercury looked genuinely impressed, 'but what if I told you where you are now there is no fixed Time, no place, no direction. You are not in the future, the present nor the past – where we are now is everywhere but it's also nowhere – in conclusion, young man, you are in the Timeless Dimension, and anything is possible here and nothing is real the way you see it – and that makes us lot all very curious as to how you did what you did last night?' The Dragon drew close to Stan and stared at him with liquid silver eyes. 'So who are you and why can you peer beyond Time and Space?'

'Um,' said Stan, 'Poppy broke my telescope?' He hadn't thought of that as an explanation until now and he wasn't really following what the Dragon was saying except for the fact that when he had looked through the telescope the night before, he had seen nothing except ... he shivered when he thought of that eye full of menace and power. He looked up and was disconcerted to find Mercury staring at him again, all traces of humour gone.

'This is more important than you can possibly imagine, Manchild. The Particle of Light has been missing for 10,000 years: if it is once more in play it could mean the end of all we know for Dragons and you Humans, too. You know what I think?

'Um ... no.'

'I think you saw us for a reason and, more importantly, I can't touch the Particle of Light. That's why I need you – only Humans can handle it, for it is part of you. To put it bluntly, I reckon we'll be needing to go back to that planet of yours to get it.'

CHAPTER V

Some Greek and Roman gods were good, some wicked.
The hard part was working out who was what.
Most just made up the rules as they went along.

Because they could.

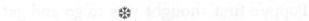

BACK ON PLANET EARTH, where Time was still taken seriously and little girls should have been fast asleep, Poppy had watched Stan walk across the garden with his telescope. She didn't know what had drawn her to open the bedroom curtains, she usually did her very best to avoid them – looking outside when it got dark was scary in case she saw a fox or a bad person outside. But she had lain in her bed trying to sleep, the borrowed crystal from Stan's collection in her hand, when a small voice in her conscience told her to get out of bed, so she obeyed. She slipped the crystal into the pocket at the front of her nightgown, shrugged out of her

sheets and went barefoot, on tippy-toes, over to the window and stared out at Stan who trod slowly across the dewy grass and then ...

vanished.

She blinked hard. A second before her brother was standing there, looking up, his head tilted strangely into the empty sky, as if he could see something she could not, the next instant there was a slight blurring in the night sky and ... he was gone.

Poppy's first thought was to go and get Mummy, who would be fast asleep in front of the TV. Then she had second thoughts: she didn't want to get Stan in trouble for a second time that day, he was still mad at her. She would go outside first and check he really was gone. He might have fallen down. Into a hole.

She paused by the front door and took a deep breath. Inside her nightdress her small heart was thumping, boom, boom, boom. Poppy reached up to the latch and twisted it, taking three or four goes to get it to turn all the way around and open with a springy click. Cooler air flooded in from the garden

and the darkness came in, too. She looked over her shoulder, checking to see if her mother would come running out of the living room: even though she was five, she still believed parents could always tell if you were doing something naughty.

But the living room door remained half open and the only movement was the television, which threw out its blurry reflection onto the stone floor in the hallway.

Poppy took a moment to get all her courage up, then stepped into the night.

She had never been outside on her own after bedtime before.

The wet grass felt funny on her bare feet and, for a moment, Poppy forgot to be scared and looked around at her familiar garden in an unfamiliar light. It even smelled different – it smelled *more*. She had never noticed but you could tell the difference between leaves and the earth and grass, all separate and nice in their own way; the only smells she had noticed before were bad (dog's breath), good (cake, strawberry felt-tips). She stepped forward, right out into the garden now, out of the reassuring half circle of light coming from the back door and looked hard, her eyes gradually adjusting to the dark.

'Stan!' she stage-whispered.

The grass around where he had been standing was flattened right down, as if something very large and very heavy had lain there. Poppy also noticed it was dry and hot, not like the rest of the lawn at all.

'STAN?' this time louder, as she saw a shape in the bushes.

'HhhgrrRRHHH.' That did not sound like the sort of thing Stan would say at all and Poppy's heart began to beat very loud and very fast all over again.

A low growl came again from under the bushes. Even when he was pretending, Stan didn't sound that big or scary. Poppy nearly turned and ran towards the safety of the half-open front door but remembered that her brother was still out there, with The Thing That Growled. She saw a stick lying at her feet and had an idea – if it was a dog she would throw the stick away and it would chase the stick, not her, and she could find Stan. She would save him!

She bent down and, as she did so, felt a warm drop of something on the back of her hand. With the stick hanging limply from her small fist, she looked up to see not two, but six red eyes burning through the dark above her and three huge mouths full of teeth. Mouths for biting.

Before she had time to draw in a breath to scream,

there was a loud thump in the air all around her and it felt as if she was being squeezed in a huge black bag, whilst her bare feet left the ground.

CHAPTER VI

Dragons come in almost unlimited type and number:
there are Water Dragons; Air Dragons; Fire Dragons;
Earth Dragons; Lizard Dragons; Worm Dragons;
Lion Dragons ...

so, why not Space Dragons?

'JUST NIPPING BACK ... right now we're bending the laws of aerodynamics, tearing up the dimensional rule book, poking fun at physics.' Mercury talked at Stan, as the Dragon's Aura took him up and they began to lift off the surface of the cave. Stan was getting used to the feeling of lightness within the Aura, similar – he imagined – to being without gravity in the International Space Station. He'd always dreamed of doing this, he thought, and he allowed himself to turn slowly, in a lazy, relaxing corkscrew – like an astronaut – the better to study the huge metallic cliffs and quicksilver waterfalls they travelled past.

'I'll aim for the time just after our last visit, then there's no chance of you bumping into yourself, which is never pleasant and usually a tough one to explain.'

'It's like Time travel, then?' asked Stan, possibilities and plans forming in his head. 'Um, that's brilliant!'

Mercury sniffed. 'Suppose it is – we do it all the time, so I don't give it much thought. It's more like opening doors ... the time bit, doesn't really count if you're more or less immortal, like us.'

'You mean you can't die?' Stan was impressed.

'Well we can die, technically, but I've never seen it. We'll grow old and eventually hide away, like some of us have already done. But we take our strength from the laws of the Universe – you lot always loved that about us ... and we loved ...' Mercury sniffed again as they carried on rising through a cathedral-like cavern, '... yes, well, enough about that ... OK!' he sounded business-like, 'going through that portal now,' as they got to the mouth of the cave. There was a slight flicker of light as if they were passing through an almost invisible elastic skin, and then they were onto the rocky surface of the planet Stan recognised from the internet as Mercury, and in their own dimension.

'My Aura will screen us from any prying eyes, but you might want to climb on my back, it means I can go faster – the sooner we get to the bottom of all this Particle stuff, the better – trust me on this.'

The journey was the same as the last one but in reverse. This time, Stan did his best to drink in every detail without falling asleep. As Mercury flew over his own planet Stan stared at the Sun, which was huge, even at this distance, at least twenty times larger than on Earth and just looking at it made him hot. Something about the Aura must have been filtering the light so it did not blind him.

'Wikipedia says that Mercury is the closest planet to the Sun and the smallest,' said Stan.

Mercury half turned as he beat his wings, flying across the surface. 'Never heard of this Wiki guy, but he's right: my planet might be small but it's the hottest and it's also the coldest,' Mercury sounded proud. 'No atmosphere – especially when I'm not there, ha, ha! Geddit? Mind you, as I was saying to an Ice Giant only the other decade or so ago, I've no idea why they put me so far away from everyone else, not in the middle of the Solar System.'

It's because you never shut up, thought Stan. 'How long's it going to take to get back to Earth?' Now they were definitely going back, he wanted to

get as much from this experience as possible. It was amazing how quickly you got used to a talking Dragon made of liquid metal and the ability to fly around the Solar System.

'Well, put it this way, I'm pretty bloody fast,' was all Mercury said, as he took a sharp bank upwards until the planet's horizon began to curve and then went into a dive, heading back towards the rocky surface. At the last moment, just when Stan was positive they would crash and die on the sharp rocks (smallish red splat = Stan; biggish silver splat = Mercury), the Dragon did two things: he veered sharply sideways, tilting one wing up, one down, now heading straight for the Sun; then he inhaled. Even through the Aura Stan felt heat building inside the Dragon, as if being sucked directly from the burning, boiling surface of the Sun that looked close enough to reach out and touch. The heat made the dragon's scales glow red, then white hot and at the last moment, Mercury opened his mouth and a twisting tower of pure silver flame shot out.

The universe around Stan blurred.

If Stan liked a subject, he could remember almost everything about it, first time. He knew that a solar flare, which was very much like the fire corridor Mercury had just created, can travel over five million miles an hour with 25,000 times more energy than a comet. Protected by Mercury from the tremendous heat, unseen by Human eyes in his Aura, they approached Earth in a blur of light, the planets and the stars streaking away from them soundlessly. Stan was quite sure he'd be sick, then he had just enough time to realise he actually felt fine, when they skidded to a halt and the silver flames disappeared.

Landing in the garden, Mercury slipped back into his own dimension, so anyone looking out of their window at 9pm on Tuesday night in Long Witten-ham, Oxfordshire, would merely have seen a boy standing in his garden, wondering if it had all been a dream.

'Told you I was quick.' A slight blurring of the night sky above Stan told him that a) he hadn't just imagined it all, and b) Mercury was right beside him.

'Um, OK,' said Stan. 'What do we do now?'

'Dunno, we take a loo—' Mercury stopped, and Stan felt the Dragon's body stiffen. Silver scales

appeared for a moment in the pale moonlight. 'Hold the phone...' Stan heard the Dragon sniff the air. 'Cerberus, if I'm not mistaken. Now, that would be interesting if it wasn't so worrying.'

'What?' said Stan, there was something in Mercury's voice that made him suddenly anxious.

'Big dog, to you, three heads and you wouldn't want to meet either of 'em ... belongs to someone ... not nice ...' Mercury took another sniff, slower and more thoughtful. There was a long silence. 'Oh, no.' More silence from the usually talkative Dragon.

Eventually Stan couldn't take it any longer. 'What?'

Mercury eyes appeared in the night, silver pools with jet black pupils. He looked concerned. 'Did you say you had a sister?'

Seconds later, Stan raced through the still half-open door, past the living room with the TV still on and up the stairs. He burst into Poppy's room and stared at her empty bed with the sheets pulled back and then at the open curtains. She must have seen him and then gone outside. Stan was alarmed, but he also felt familiar annoyance rise up. *Poppy!* She was ruining everything, yet again.

He went to his room, to double check she wasn't there. It was empty, so he turned to go —

'What are you doing still up?'

Stan froze, his fingers on the door handle. 'Oh, hi, Mum,' he said, trying to sound casual, but his mind racing. 'I was just about to go to bed now.' He did his best to look as if he had been just about to go into, not out of his room.

'Well, it may be the holidays but ten thirty is far too late, your father would have a fit.'

Stan saw that his mother looked half asleep, so she probably hadn't noticed yet that he was fully dressed. In his experience the first thirty seconds were crucial, then he had to make himself scarce. His mother yawned and turned. 'I'll just go and check on your sister.'

GaaaaahhhHHH! Went Stan's brain. 'That's fine!' A bit squeaky, but at least his mother stopped, 'I already went in, just now ... to see if she was alright.'

His mum blinked. 'What?'

'I went in to check on her ...' Stan was grasping at straws but at least she hadn't gone in, '... and to say sorry ... um, if she was still awake.' One good thing about never saying much was that no one suspected Stan of telling fibs when he did get around to talking.

His mother paused and half smiled, 'well, that's

nice, but I'm sure she's been fast asleep for ages, as should you be,' she started to walk back past Stan to her room at the other end of the corridor. 'Goodnight, then.'

'Goodnight, Mum,'

'And tomorrow we'll do something nice, all three of us.'

'Oh. Great.'

❄

Stan's head was reeling as he went back into his room and started making fake going-to-bed noises. His sister had vanished and instead of telling his mother, who would call his father, the police, his grandparents and probably the Prime Minister, he was keeping it quiet, just so he could go back into Space with a Dragon he'd only just met.

No, that was wrong – he was keeping quiet so they could find her, get her back safely and...

'Where's my sister!' he almost shouted at Mercury when he got back into the garden. It had taken his mother ages to change, brush her teeth, faff about in the spare room for some reason, then finally go to bed and put the light out. 'She's incredibly annoying, but Mum and Dad like her.'

'I won't lie to you, I haven't got the foggiest.' Mercury seemed agitated. If he'd been a Human and visible, he would have been hopping from one foot to the other. 'I know who nabbed her, if that helps?'

'That dog?'

'Cerberus – yeah, sure of it. Not sure why. And the Particle of Light isn't here. It was recently, but it's gone, like your sister.'

'Sorry, you're saying this three-headed dog took my sister?' Stan had a sudden horrible thought, 'it won't eat her, will it?'

'Naaah,' Mercury tried to sound casual. 'Might chew her a bit, if she's the wriggly sort of Human – a lot of you lot are, as it happens.'

'What?!'

'Anyway,' the Dragon added hastily, 'that big doggie never acts on its own – he'll have been sent.'

'Who by?' asked Stan.

'Hades, of course.'

Stan went through his memory. 'That's the other name for Pluto. Wasn't that a planet, but now everyone says it's not?'

'I hadn't heard that one,' Mercury sounded worried, 'just another reason for him to hate everyone even more. Hades' rock is pretty far out, as far as you can go in the Solar System and he's real enough

and ... well I'm just a messenger and so now I've got to go and tell someone who'll know what to do about the Particle of Light, Cerberus and what Hades might be up to.'

'What's that?'

'Sorry, I can't say, not until we've talked to a few of my kind.'

'OK, I'll come,' Stan surprised himself. He never volunteered for anything.

'No.'

'What? But you said I smell of this Particle of Light thing and that I saw you for a reason...' he stopped suddenly, out of the corner of his eye, Stan saw the beside light go on in his mother's room. His mother was a light sleeper. Aggh! If she came downstairs and found him in the garden ... he wasn't sure he could think of something quick enough to explain what he was doing. He'd have to tell her about Poppy. He turned back to Mercury, 'Really, I can help.'

'Definitely not, times ten ... every time Humans get involved with our affairs, things get out of hand.'

Stan saw her mother's silhouette sit up in bed. Her outline moved towards the window. Stan's heart thudded in his chest. Then he turned and

looked at Poppy's dark window. The curtains were half open, and even from there the room felt cold and empty.

She was so little.

Scenes with Poppy when they were younger flashed through his mind: Poppy laughing and splashing in her bath when Stan made fart noises with his armpits; Stan showing Poppy how to make a Lego Tyrannosaurus Rex; sitting close together watching the rain sweep across the lawn from the shelter of a camp they made at the bottom of the garden, feeling safe and snug. She held his hand – she was always holding his hand in those days, because he let her. And he didn't mind. Not really. He took a deep breath. 'Look, we need to leave right now. If I don't find my sister...' He knew that he wanted to say all the stuff he'd just thought of, but he was worried it would sound stupid to a Dragon; so he said something else. 'Um ... I'll get all the blame – Mum will say it's all my fault and she'll tell Dad...'

Mercury brought his face close to Stan, so he could feel his breath, very hot on his forehead. 'I'm a bit out of practice with your kind and never had much to do with kids, but don't you mean, *I insist on coming with you to rescue my sister, wot is only small*

61

and helpless and is probably scared half to death?'

Stan, who was swiftly coming to the conclusion that immortal Dragons could be as bad as adults when it came to lecturing you, decided not to say anything that might make it worse, so he just nodded.

'Well...' Mercury still looked very doubtful. 'OK, you can come for now ... then we'll see what She has to say, but we'll have to hurry.'

Stan saw his mother reach for the curtain.

'Okgreatletsgo.'

VENUS

Age: *4 million years*
Size: *12 tonnes*
Body made of: *Gems and minerals
(ruby, diamond, sapphire and cobalt)*

Fire: *Purple (she would say
'mauveine, darling')*

CHAPTER VII

Light speed is the fastest speed ever recorded.
It is equal to travelling 671 million miles an hour.
HOWEVER, *even at that speed,*
it would take you 46.5 billion years
just to get to the edge of the part
of the Universe we can see with a telescope.

❄

IF STAN HAD THOUGHT the fire corridor going back to Earth was fast, this was a whole new experience. He didn't know it at the time, but in the few moments that followed, he didn't just break the record for how fast a living Human had ever travelled: he smashed it, then trod the pieces into the carpet of history.

Mercury was obviously in a hurry to share his news with whomever he needed to tell. Up until that day (although they had just left any idea of days, hours, minutes – Time – far behind them), Stan would have found it hard to imagine a Dragon

65

panicking. However, Mercury was definitely panicking.

This alone should have caused Stan to worry. Had he not been able to get his head around anything other than the speed they were going. No sooner had he felt the familiar Aura envelop him than Mercury extended his neck and sent a jet of white-hot fire into the sky, so bright Stan had to close his eyes and, even then, the mercury flare burned against his closed lids until he saw red, not black. As the flaming jet stream punched through the night sky, he was torn off the ground, out of the Earth's comforting atmosphere and into the Fastest Human Ever record books.

Though they now travelled close to the speed of light, it still felt safe, cocooned in the warm, springy air of the Aura, and silent. As usual, Mercury filled the silence.

'So I said "It'll only wrap itself around your head if you try and fight a Hydra wearing that thing and you'll get yourself digested ... slowly – give yourself a chance Hercs and, anyway, togas are so First Century" – so he goes off in a huff but he comes back later when he's calmed down with this kind of nappy and I'm like "are you taking the Poseidon?" and he's like "mumble, mumble ... no" – you'd get

on, you two – and I'm like "well Hercy, I guess you're going to have a career whatever you wear – you're a demigod, after all ... fiends in high places, ha ha" ...'

Stan had largely zoned out and was lost, as usual, in his own thoughts. If he had to guess what a Dragon might be like; if a teacher had asked him in class or it had been a question on TV, he'd have used words like *scary*, *gigantic*, *strong* ... *fiery*. The point being, *talkative* wouldn't have been one of the words. Or *slightly annoying*. It was like being stuck in a car listening to local radio.

He zoned out again and looked around. 'Wow,' he said under his breath.

In Space, the Fire Corridor's sides were transparent, like a jet fighter's thrusters at full speed. Without the glare, he could open his eyes properly, without squinting and study the rapidly disappearing blue and green ball of the Earth as well as the stars themselves. Not for the first time did Stan wonder at how he was taking all this so calmly – he supposed it was only a few years ago that he really did believe his mum when she said there was a troll at the bottom of the garden living under the well stone, so talking Dragons was not too much of a leap. To be fair, it was only the bit of the last twelve hours with Dragons in it which was so unusual: the

planets had always been real enough.

After only a few minutes, a very bright dot in front of them seemed to be getting a lot bigger. Stan watched in wonder as the shiny coin in a sea of black became larger, opaque white and fuzzier, as if surrounded by clouds.

'I know where we're going!' said Stan uncharacteristically excited.

Mercury jumped, startled that Stan had said something. 'Ooh, hark at him – know your planets, then, Manchild?'

'Sure,' said Stan, 'this one's easy – the brightest planet in the solar system, and the closest to Earth, but even then that's over a hundred million miles, which means ...'

' ... we're in a rush. We're moving just about as fast as I can go. Brisk dawdle, that was before, now we're up to fast panicky.'

'A hundred million miles an hour!' Stan easily did the calculation – partly because he'd always been good at maths, partly because it was easy ... then he thought about it and felt excited and sick at the same time. 'But Venus is covered in volcanoes, it's got sulphuric acid for clouds and so much pressure you'd be squashed to the size of a coin if you tried to get out of your spaceship.'

'You know so much. You really have come along way, as a species,' Mercury seemed almost sad, 'since you lost us.'

'Lost you?'

'Yup, 'fraid so,' replied the Dragon, slowing visibly; the silver Fire Corridor narrowed and began to curve down, as the planet filled their vision. Mercury spoke more gravely now, as if from memory, using someone else's words. 'There was a time,' he recited, 'when we were as gods to you and you were our favourites of all the species in the firmament. When we settled in this system, we watched how you looked to the stars; you saw our eight fires, one for each of our home planets, and how each was different and you worshipped us as gods. In return we loved you and protected you. We gave you the gifts of flight and fire, and elevated some of you to almost equals – Perseus, Hercules, Orpheus, Theseus ... they ruled on Earth and explored the heavens on our scaled backs.' The Dragon now turned and stared at Stan from deep within the liquid silver of his eyes. 'Do you share the destiny of the heroes Manchild?' There was a long silence, as it dawned on Stan he was expected to answer.

After a long pause he said, 'Um, no, I don't think so, Miss Thorn, 5B's teacher, thinks I'm a bit lazy.'

Mercury gave him an odd look, almost back to his usual self. 'But you saw us, which makes you a very rare Human indeed. Even without the Particle of Light in your keeping.'

Stan didn't believe that for a second but, before he could say anything, the bright glare of Venus eclipsed even Mercury's fire as they hit the planet's atmosphere and were immediately enveloped in a thick fog. The sulphuric acid in the boiling clouds sizzled against the Aura, a bellowing storm billowing about them; swirls of white, then red as clouds parted to reveal a half-formed landscape of lava flows running into huge seas of molten magma and charred rock.

After circling the top of the planet, they eventually landed at the base of a volcano that towered above them. It was at least twice the height of any mountain Stan even thought possible. Its sides were sloped like a pyramid, ending in a peak that gave off a corkscrewing plume of black smoke all the way to the canopy of yellow, sulphuric fog. Stan stared about at an utterly alien landscape.

'Interesting fact: this is more or less what your Earth looked like when it was very young,' said Mercury. Every so often the ground shook with a tremor, and although he felt reasonably safe inside

the Aura, Stan moved a few steps closer to the Dragon who seemed unconcerned by all the geology in motion.

The acid fog parted and Stan saw they were standing at the mouth of a huge cave. 'What do we do now?' he asked.

'She's mysterious,' Mercury said quietly, and Stan guessed he was talking about the Dragon, the one through the telescope. 'You've seen her once, she'll be watching us, deciding. She'll know I'm carrying a message, which means she'll come. Eventually. After making us wait. Women.'

'Can you tell me more?'

'More what?'

'About the stuff you were saying before.' Stan wasn't quite sure he believed the Dragon, as yet, but it was still interesting, and although he wouldn't admit it, it was good to have something take his mind off the rivers of lava that oozed molten liquid just a bit too close to where they stood. Worry made Stan positively talkative. 'You said that you lost us. What does that mean?'

'It was the Titans, really, and they nearly destroyed everything. Hades let them in. Huge they were, your Moon is the skull of one of their kind. They get their strength from this Dark Matter all

around us: strongest thing in the Universe, some say, why bother fighting it?'

'Why did Hades let them in?'

'We've all got jobs – I'm a messenger, as you know, Mars the warrior, Venus ... yeah well, you're a bit young for all that, Jupiter's in charge and Hades got the Underworld.'

'You mean where dead people go?'

'Yeah, some call it Hell. I call it Deadly ... geddit? No? SERIOUSLY? Suit yourself.' Mercury sniffed. 'Anyway, stuck out at the end of the Solar System, he went a bit funny in the head, started talking to all this Dark Matter, got a bit pally and with their help he called up the Titans; insult to injury, they were originally made from bits of us – scales, claws ... bit of Uranus,' Mercury paused and grinned hopefully again, but Stan just looked at him, '... and this Dark Matter for power. Our great-grandfather made them, didn't much like his handiwork, but who can blame him – children with fifty heads and a taste for eating gods, so he sent them to the far reaches of the universe. Until they came back, wanting our jobs.

'And so we fought over the prize in the Solar System, the only planet with its own life, the jewel of the system, Eden – Earth. And they nearly won.

Some say they did really, because you lot now saw we weren't gods after all and could be beaten and you turned your backs on us, found new gods, better ones, that looked more like you. Hades was banished and the Titans sent back to the pit of Deep Space.'

'How did you win?'

'At our darkest hour, people were dying and we could not save them – we were exhausted, our flanks burned and hacked to raw flesh, wings in tatters and the seas aflame for thousands of leagues ... then part of a star fell to Earth. Pretty much out of nowhere. Nobody could have been more surprised than me, and I'm meant to know everything. It was a gift. Some say from a real god.'

'Yes, *indeeeeed*.' The new voice came from above them, pouring like treacle down the rock face. To Stan, it sounded like comfort and danger all rolled into one. He looked up to see that another Dragon had appeared without them noticing. She was about twice the size of Mercury.

'Oh, hello, Venus, long time,' said Mercury, his silver looking pinkish. 'See ... told you,' he whispered to Stan out of the corner of his mouth. 'You haven't aged a day,' he added, turning back to the new arrival. Venus pretended to ignore him, but

Stan could see she was pleased at the compliment.

This new Dragon's scales looked more like brightly coloured feathers and they rustled in the scorching winds whipped up by the volcanoes. Definitely female, her eyes were heavy lidded and two ridges of bone arched above them, dark and thick. They were the very same ones Stan had seen two nights before in his broken telescope.

He shuddered – as long as he lived, Stan would never forget those eyes.

If Mercury was molten metal, this creature was colour, like a firework going off: feathered and stately, she padded across the rocks and stood above them. She reminded Stan of the kind of old lady who wore too much make up and perfume and whose clothes always seemed to be competing for attention with each other. The she-dragon arched her long neck and blew out a whip of violet flame that lassoed around their heads. Stan ducked instinctively, everything obscured for a moment in white smoke, which slowly cleared and Stan could see a picture painted in lingering smoke and fire – a world at war, fires everywhere and small figures running. She stared at Stan. 'Your kind have always hungered for stories. Only a few of you can see as we do, with our own eyes and even less have travel-

led as we have. Stories are how you understand, so listen Manchild!

'The Titans had made the Earth a living hell, an abyss like the one of heat and darkness they came from. Then, when it looked certain we would lose, part of the Star fell to Earth. Your kind tell of a great flood – this was just part of the destruction it wrought. It wiped out many of the lesser Earth Dragons you call dinosaurs. The Titans, those who were not destroyed in the blast, fled back to Deep Space. For they are darkness – the Particle is light. We Dragons understand the Chaos for we are made of fire and fury; but your kind come from the stars, from the same matter as the Sun and it gave you life. This is why only Humans can touch it.' She had a deep voice, like someone who smoked too many cigarettes, which Stan supposed she sort of did. Without warning, her face suddenly shot down, huge eyes, nostrils flaring, and Stan found himself staring into the eyes he had seen from his bedroom window. He had never been so scared in all his life. 'Where is the Particle of Light, I wonder?'

'That makes two of us,' Mercury said, sounding a bit on edge himself.

'Have you asked him?'

'Well, he doesn't say much.' Those eyes whipped

around once more at Stan who found when he looked into them he pretty much forgot everything.

'Well, young man?'

'I dunno,' was really all he could think of saying.

Venus turned her mega gaze on Mercury. 'Is he a simpleton?'

'Don't *think* so,' said Mercury, as if he'd already given it some proper thought. 'Matter of fact, I think he might even be brighter than your average, or they've come a long way ... bit of both, I'm guessing.'

'Well, Manchild, the Particle of Light is deep within you, I can *taste* it ... it's power is in your flesh, your bones, your very marrow.'

Stan didn't like where this was going.

'Your fate, and that of all life on Earth, is written in the same stuff of life, for those who know how to read it. The Particle of Light is the missing part of the most important star in our Solar System and the Titans will hear its call and come. They will return for vengeance, to finish the destruction they started. So, where is the Particle, tell me do, little Manchild, open your heart ... to *me*.'

Stan noticed that now her tone had changed: she positively purred the words; her eyes softened and, in an instant, he forgot about the fires that sur-

rounded him, the deadly clouds of acid and her teeth like razors the size of broadswords. He still felt a strong desire to run away, but an even stronger feeling made him want to stay. Forever. Stan had no idea what part of a star or Particle of Light the two Dragons had been talking about. At that moment, lost in her eyes that seemed to tell him he was the centre of her universe, the whole universe in fact, he no longer felt scared of Venus, just bitterly disappointed he could not give her an answer. And uneasy at what might happen if he did not.

'Venus ...' Mercury's voice cut across the spell. 'He's just a pup, too young for your tricks.'

Venus' gaze did not leave his or so much as flicker. Her own Aura seemed to be squeezing Mercury out and wrapping itself around Stan like a mothers' arms. Or something. It made Stan feel funny. 'We need to know.'

'His sister is missing.'

Venus' neck whipped around. 'Ahhh ... who has her, is she ... like this boy? Can she see us?' Now Venus had pulled her gaze from Stan: released from it, he felt like he could breathe again.

'If you let me get a word in edgeways, I would have said,' grumbled Mercury. 'Not much of a messenger

if I'm not allowed to speak.'

There was a silence.

'Well?' Venus seemed to be smiling – at least a row of startling white fore-fangs had appeared.

'Well, indeed,' Mercury still seemed a bit sulky, and Stan wondered if it was anything to do with the sort of magic Venus seemed to give off in her Aura. 'Cerberus took the sister, I could pick up on the Hound all over their dwelling,' he shrugged. 'That's all I know.'

'And how could this Manchild ...' Venus looked at Stan, 'this *Stan* see us? Is he like the ancient ones who rode with us?'

'No,' said Stan, feeling like he wanted her attention again. All to himself. 'Poppy broke my telescope ... well she dropped it and something happened to it inside, that's how I saw you. And then Poppy stole my crystal ...' Stan stopped ... *the crystal! There was definitely something about it: Granny wouldn't say where it came from, it was always warm ... could it be ...?*

Before he had time to say anything, Venus turned to Mercury. 'Well, does this explain anything?'

'Nah, don't buy this broken tele*what*sit story,' said Mercury, 'I thought about it on the way over. But, I'll say this, it's just like the Fates to throw up

heroes when you're least expecting them, even now – keeps those old witches in the game, plus they just love it when someone unlikely is chosen. This one here doesn't look like much, I grant you that ...'

'*Hey!*' said Stan.

'... and his clothes seem a bit ... unheroey, but even Hercules didn't look the part before he grew into himself.' Mercury looked at Venus, who smiled. 'Remember – all knees and sandals?'

'I do,' she turned to Stan, smiling in that way of hers that made him feel like he was wearing an extra jumper, 'so are you a hero, Particle of Light child? Is it your great future that the patterns in the heavens have foretold?' Stan had absolutely nothing to say to this, so he looked at his feet. Mercury cut in again.

'All we know right now is that Hades' Hound is on the loose, so they'll both be up to mischief out there in the blackness.'

'Then, it is a matter for Dragons, take this Human child back, we have everything we need to know from him, you did well to bring him.'

'I'm not going back.' Stan was surprised how sure he sounded.

'I've been through this with him already. He's

barely a mouthful, but he's surprisingly stubborn. Go on, you try to tell him.'

Venus turned, looking serious. 'Stan. This may seem like an adventure but even the strongest Humans with a great destiny have fallen when we Dragons go to war. Before we know who you really are, it is too dangerous. You are just a child.'

'But I saw you, didn't I?'

'That may be so, but even if the Fates have picked you out as a new hero, you have too much to learn before you can help us rescue your sister. We do not have enough time to teach you.'

'You said the future of Humans rests on whether we save my sister and get this Particle back ... well I'm the only Human you've got and Poppy is my sister and it's our world in danger.'

'He's got a point,' Mercury said quietly, 'the fate of this mess is as much to do with them as us, remember, only they can touch the Particle of Light, to carry it back to where it belongs.'

'But we are the gods, not them!'

'Only because we *let* you be gods. We invented that.' Stan shut his mouth, wondering if he'd just gone too far.

But Venus didn't fry him on the spot. In fact, she did not answer at all, instead she turned away and

looked upwards. It took Stan a few moments to realise she was studying the stars.

'I can see his path is very long, but his destiny is unclear,' she said eventually, 'he has so far to go, and so little time ... but he has ... something ... perhaps he will become the hero he could be and perhaps in time for when he is needed. But it is uncertain.'

'So?' Mercury leaned forward. There was a long pause.

'So ... I suppose take him we must.'

Mercury winked at Stan, who couldn't help smiling.

'But we need to assemble the Council,' Venus looked unconcerned, but the suggestion seemed to worry Mercury.

'I was hoping you weren't going to say that. It's been over ten thousand years – and we're not as young as we once were...' then he caught the expression on Venus' face, 'except you of course!'

'You're too kind ... of course, we'll have to stop by Mars, on our way to see Him.'

'What, that lunatic? Are you quite sure about that?'

Venus blew a plume of smoke in Mercury's face, making him cough. 'Oh, I'm sure he's mellowed, like

us all. If the Girlchild has the missing piece of the Star, and the Hound or even Hades himself has her, we need to get to them before they work out a way of getting it from her. The Hound won't know how to use it, but the Lord of the Underworld will. Mars is on our way,' Venus fluttered her eyelashes and Mercury caught Stan's eye, and shrugged the merest fraction. 'And we might need protecting, the stars suggest Hades will send forces to meet us. We have to cross the River of Rock.'

Venus inhaled to the full extent of her huge lungs, raised her neck and shot out a jet of deep violet flame. 'We fly now, and we fly together, Dragon and Human for the first time in ten millennia, to save our world and theirs!'

'You're the boss,' said Mercury, and his silver fire joined Venus'.

❄

As they roared up through the planet's atmosphere Stan had a question. Two, in fact.

'Mercury?' he said.

The Dragon turned around, pretending to be startled. 'By the gods, he speaks before spoken to! Hope it's interesting.'

'Was Venus really reading the stars? I thought that stuff was all made up.'

'Everything is out there, young Stan, all the answers are for the seeing, you just need to know where to look.'

'But how does she do it?'

'Good eyesight! No seriously,' Mercury added, when he saw the look on Stan's face. 'We Dragons have been reading the stars for millions of years. You are Earth-bound and you do not have our vision, so you can only see what is visible from your planet. For you there are a piffling twelve signs and twelve houses, around one sun. It's like trying to work out what a Unicorn is just by looking at the end of its tail. But a Dragon can see deep into Space, just in this galaxy alone there are two billion more suns, each with their own houses and there are a trillion galaxies beyond this one. A Dragon can read this and tell not just your future but the galaxies echo the past and present.'

Stan took a deep breath. Here goes, he thought. 'I think my crystal, that Poppy took, is the Particle of Light.'

Mercury looked at him. 'Unlike most humans, you're not as stupid as you look ... same thing crossed my mind when you mentioned it earlier.'

'If Poppy has it?'

'The Particle of Light – and let's hope she still does, for all our sakes.'

'OK... um ... what will they do, to get it?'

Mercury turned and looked at Stan, his eyes grave. 'You mean, you're finally actually a bit concerned?'

Stan shrugged: why did everyone keep expecting him to say embarrassing things. 'I guess.'

'Look, Hades hates your kind, if he can get his horrible, black claws on the missing piece, it could destroy us all and he's a bit bonkers – although what do you expect from someone who only gets to go around the Sun once in two hundred and forty-eight years. In the wrong hands, the Particle of Light would mean the end of this Solar System, us and even you. He won't risk that, but he will use the missing piece of the Star we call the Particle of Light and your sister to get what he wants.'

'What's that?'

'Oh, the usual bad guy stuff. He wants revenge; if you asked him, he'd probably say he wants Jupiter's power and us to bow to him. But he's not just evil and a bit barmy: he's clever. I think he just wants to make us all sorry for not being nicer to him. I won't lie to you, he risked destroying the Solar System ten

thousand years ago when he set the Titans against us. A little thing like your sister in his way won't give him a moment's hesitation.'

'Then you've got to do something!'

'No, Stan,' Mercury looked serious, 'you're with us now, so that means we've got to do something.' Stan wasn't sure if he was joking or not. 'There's one thing that's in our favour, though.'

'What's that?' Stan was pleased for any ray of hope.

'If he touches any part of the Particle, it'll destroy him, immortal or not, on any dimension he cares to try. And he knows that.'

'What's he going to do, then?'

'He'll try to trick your sister into using it against us and you Humans, is my best guess, he's sly like that.' Mercury shook his head, 'But I'm just a humble messenger, what do I know?' He paused. 'This missing Particle of Light holds power. When the main part of it fell to Earth, it burned up but we always knew some small piece lay hidden on Earth. We should have tried to find it, but after the war was over and you turned your backs on us and went off and worshipped other gods, we sort of left you to it. I guess we were sulking.'

'Really?'

'Yes, really. Humans were right about one thing – we're very powerful but we aren't gods: we bicker and fight amongst ourselves and we can sulk for millennia. And hold a grudge – look at Hades. If anything, you're the ones who are special, especially you Stan. The fact that you can handle the Star in its solid form, something that would kill us instantly, must mean something.'

'Do we have a plan?' In Stan's world, plans were important.

Mercury looked doubtful. 'It'll depend on what Jupiter says and if we can get there – Venus wasn't joking, it's a dangerous journey. But if we join the missing Particle of Light to the Mother Star, the Titans will never be able to come back, we'll all be safe. If Hades figures out a way to destroy it, the Mother Star will die.'

'What's the Mother Star?'

'Look behind you.'

Stan turned and stared at the burning giant world in the sky that was larger than anything: in Space it seemed even hotter, more blazing and vital. He looked back at Mercury. 'The Sun?'

Mercury smiled. 'Now you're beginning to get it.'

❄

EPISODE

I t was dark and cold, and Poppy stared out into the blackness as hard as she could but saw nothing. Wherever she was, it felt like a very, very long way away from home. And not for the first (or last) time in a few hours, she wanted to cry. Her bottom lip quivered when she heard the big dog, close by, growl. She swallowed. Her throat ached from screaming for help and she was very thirsty.

The last thing she remembered, before waking up in this freezing place where she couldn't see anything, was the monster dog with three heads coming towards her and then a blinding flash of light before she went sort of wobbly and

fainted.

Stan will come, she kept telling herself. Stan will come and rescue me ... if he's not still cross about the telescope.

Somewhere, even through her fear, she registered that her kidnapper wasn't happy either. From time to time it would whine as if in pain, and once, when she felt it come closer, it yelped and jumped back, as if she hurt it. The only warmth – in fact, the only scrap of comfort – came from the crystal in her pocket.

But Poppy didn't have time to try to figure it out. She stared up with large eyes at a spot that had just appeared in the distance.

Something even darker than the black fog all around her was coming.

MARS

Age: *4 million years*
Size: *6 tonnes*
Body made of: *Rock*
Fire: *Blood Red*

CHAPTER VIII

Hard to believe it,
but Mars was the second most important
god to the Romans after Jupiter:
not only the Roman god of war,
he was also the father of
Romulus and Remus, the founders of Rome.

❄

'ANNIHILATE THEM, I SAY, smash 'em to bits with big rocks 'n' stuff, corkscrew their eyeballs, spit in their food!'

Mars, like the planet he lived on, was red and rocky. He looked like he had been carved out of roughly cut granite and spray painted the same colour as a postbox.

'Get two thunderbolts, tie them to their pants when they're sleeping and blast them into Outa Space. It'll get rid of 'em and give them a wedgie at the same time.'

'Well, someone's definitely mellowed,' said Mer-

cury, giving Venus a look.

'Dahhrrling,' Venus ignored the silver Dragon, striding forward, her wings stretched out behind her giving her the look of a brightly-coloured ship in full sail. 'You look as magnificent as ever ... oh, my! Have you been working out? MWAAH!'

'Hmpphhrr,' and Mars went even redder, if that was possible, and steam poured from his ears. 'Yes, well ... like to keep meself in shape ... so, tell me about this problem you've got and why you've come to me.' He clearly was more comfortable discussing monsters and maniacs than being kissed by Venus. So far, they'd only told Mars there was a bit of trouble brewing, to explain why they had turned up uninvited, and he'd jumped on a large rock and started to rant.

So, Mercury told him the whole story, whilst Stan looked around the planet, hoping to see signs of one of the Mars Rovers from Earth. After Mercury had finished there was a long silence. They all watched in alarm as Mars' face sort of bunched up and his cheeks went purple. The steam coming out of his ears started to whistle just like a kettle.

'WHAAAAAATT!!!!! Stealing little girls, meddling with forces greater than the Cosmos, threatening the future of all life, breaking telescopes...'

'Poppy did that,' Stan felt obliged to set the record straight.

'Poppy!!! Who is this foul creature in league with the forces of darkness?'

'That's my sister,' replied Stan, glad that finally someone was taking the whole business about coming into his room seriously.

'The one Cerberus snatched up in his jaws and took somewhere in the Outer Reaches? You don't look too worried, if you ask me.'

'— he internalises,' Mercury stepped in, 'unlike someone else,' he added under his breath.

'What's that?' Evidently having piping hot water coming out of your ears did nothing for your hearing.

Venus felt the need to put them back on track. 'Anyway, the fact remains, we've got a huge problem and it involves us all. We're off to see Him. Will you come?'

'What *Him*, him?' asked Mars who looked worried, all of a sudden.

'Quite, but we need your help to get there.'

'Er ...' Mars had gone from red to pale pink. 'Well, um ... been a bit under the weather recently ...'

'What's wrong with Mars?' Stan whispered to Mercury, pretty sure the red Dragon would not

overhear. 'Isn't Mars supposed to be the god of war? He shouldn't be scared of anything.'

'Lots to do around here...' Mars seemed to be trying to think up excuses, '... there's some stray meteorites off Capricorn that need crushing and there's been talk of Gorgons – they don't smite themselves, you know ... '

'Jupiter makes him nervous,' Mercury whispered back, 'always has. And as well he should – Jupiter is the most powerful one of us, but it's not really that – old Mars here will fight anyone, but he's not exactly clever. Jupiter makes him feel stupid – the old boy can be a bit superior, it has to be said. Bit of an intellectual snob is Jupiter. So, poor old Mars here has always avoided him.'

'Pleeeaaase, Daddy will be delighted to see you,' said Venus, fluttering her lashes at the small but muscular Dragon, 'we need your help to cross the Asteroid Belt and if Cerberus is about, who knows what else is wandering around the system?'

'Well, I ...um ... I ... suppose I might be able ... '

'Great, so that settles it, then!' said Mercury brightly.

Mars looked alarmed but recovered quickly. He grinned at Stan with teeth like a mouthful of guillotines. 'Not quite ... What say you, young Human?

I'm sure my brother and sister here are all for dropping you off at the next habitable planet, where you'll be safe.'

'Already tried that,' Mercury interjected. 'It seems his Summer Holidays – whatever they are – were a bit too boring, so he would rather save the universe. Say what you like about Humans: for a species that dies over virtually every little thing, some of them don't half look for trouble.'

'Well, then,' Mars continued, 'you have a destiny! All humans will be counting on you. By gods, if I wasn't completely red, I'd be green with jealousy! Crossing the River of Rock will be full of peril – a great adventure! Will you fight with us?'

'Yes?' Stan looked at the sanest person he could think of, but Mercury just shrugged.

'We told you it would be dangerous.'

'But your parents will be proud of you.' Venus added with a smile.

Stan thought about it. Not so much proud but coming home with his sister still meant a lot less explaining than without. And Stan was all for keeping explaining to a minimum. 'I guess I can do a tiny bit of fighting,' he said doubtfully

'OUTSTANDING!' cried Mars, 'That's good enough for me, what are we waiting for?'

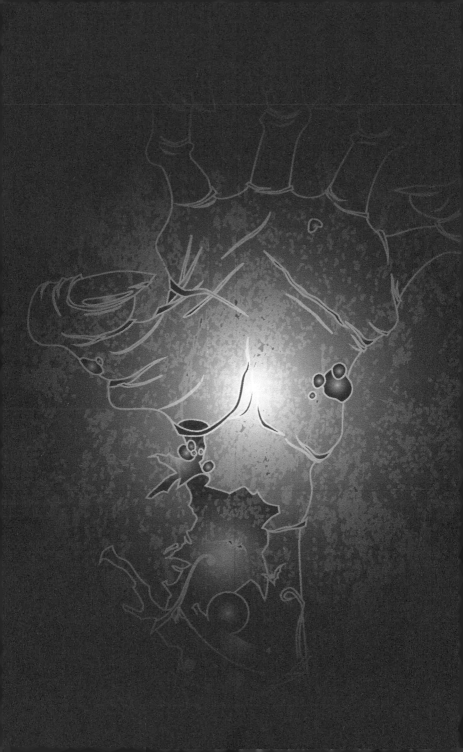

CHAPTER IX

*The Main Asteroid Belt is a barrier of ice and rock
between the orbits of the Young Planets:
Mars, Venus, Mercury ... the Earth
and the Old: Jupiter, Saturn, Neptune
... and Hades*

❄

AND SO, BEFORE LONG, they were back in orbit,
sling-shotting around Mars' gravitational pull, before firing upwards: Mercury's silver fire con-
trasting with the dark red furnace of Mars and the
deep purple of Venus. Earth was just a tiny speck
that Stan could scarcely pick out amongst all the
other points of light in the huge, revolving chart of
Space all around. Venus, who had taken Stan up in
her aura for this leg of the journey, watched him
looking at the fading dot of his home. 'It really is
the most beautiful thing for light years. And I
should know, when I was much younger and, well,
more adventurous shall we say,

I travelled the length the Galaxy and never saw anything to match the variety, its ...' she paused and took a deep breath, 'its LIFE.'

'I think your planet is a cool planet,' said Stan, thinking about the volcanoes with more fondness now they were several hundred thousand miles away.

Venus smiled at this. 'But, aside from all the drama – all that geology – they are really just empty lumps of rock or balls of gas. And lonely too.' She looked sad. 'But your Earth is unique, you are unique as a species – so like the gods you took us for in so many ways, but you make mistakes like children. We have looked after you, grieved when you have destroyed each other or killed other life on the planet, but we've also been amazed at your kindness, your goodness and your strength. You are flawed and fascinating.'

'What does that mean?'

'My dahhrrling, take it from a silly old thing with not much in her life anymore – it means you're worth saving. I could see it in your eyes when Mercury said you might be special, I know you don't believe him, but ...' she stopped and smiled at him. 'I think you may surprise us all.'

'Mmm,' said Stan.

'Mars may be a bit ... rough around the edges, but we could well be grateful for his assistance – we have to cross the Great River of Rock and whatever lurks there worries me – I've read signs in the sky these last few days. I don't see things as clearly as my grandfather, Saturn, but I've learned to read the stars over the millennia and I feel it in my scales, trouble is ahead – I'm rarely wrong. Look!'

Stan stared out across the vast velvety blackness and saw a faint line of grey. It got larger after a few minutes and he was able to make out a flat belt of millions of rocks, just like a huge river that flowed to infinity: this was the field of asteroids Venus spoke about, thousands of miles across, stretching in a huge curve as far as the eye could see and beyond.

In a flurry of flapping silver, Mercury burst into Venus' aura. He seemed more than usually jumpy. 'Did you see that? Oh gods, I hope I was imagining it. I was just flying along, then I'm sure I saw something, out of the corner of my eye, it was, sort of a dark shape, then it went away and then I LOOKED AGAIN ...'

'Mercury.'

' ... and there was something ...'

'Mercury!'

'What? What's that, why?'

'Shh.'

'Don't *shush* me ...'

'Then how about *you're right, shhh*?' Venus was staring hard ahead.

'I'm always right,' Mercury looked pleased, then suddenly worried. 'Right about what?'

'We are being attacked! Gods! This is sooner than expected – our brother Hades really means war.' Venus turned to Stan: 'Stay close, Manchild.'

Ahead of them, Mars had obviously seen something, too. He banked and sent out a jet of blood-red flame. As he did so, Stan saw a movement amongst the gathering of the asteroids nearest them, something ragged, like a living scarecrow, jumped between the rocks then hid out of sight.

Stan looked as hard as he could, trying to peer through the shimmering Aura at what Venus could see. Even Mercury stopped talking for once and scanned the lines of rocks that drifted silently towards them, their tops shrouded in ice.

'Uh ... oh,' he murmured. 'I think I know what that was.'

'What?' asked Stan, feeling the first twinges of real fear since this all began. He blinked and stared hard at the rocks in the inky blackness.

Mercury looked at Stan. 'Only, I really, really hope

I'm wrong –'

Once again, a burst of Mars' fire lit up the area and threw out a huge flapping shadow as another ragged shape danced across the surface of the nearest boulder. The belt of rocks loomed around them now: a silent, drifting army, some the size of cars, others as large as a hill.

'Unfortunately, it doesn't look like you are wrong,' said Venus.

Mars, now some way to their left, hastily shot off in the direction of another shadow, leaving them in virtual darkness, screened from the stars by the rocks that crowded in on them from all sides.

Venus and Mercury flew on carefully, with Stan in the larger Dragon's Aura. It was as if they were creeping down a haunted corridor of granite: chunks of dirty ice clung to the rock like the remains of flesh on bone. Mercury decided the time was right to send out a small but continuous burst of silver flame to light their passage, as a series of shapes on all sides jumped back. Something behind them moved. Stan realised how vulnerable they were. He played a lot of computer games and this felt like they were walking into a trap. 'Can't we go over the asteroids?' he whispered.

'There is no top, this is a more of a wall than a

river, so through is our only choice.' Both Dragons were taut with expectation, their great sinews and muscles bunched and strained in anticipation of a fight.

'What are they?'

'It's Hades,' said Mercury, as if talking to himself, not taking his eyes off the asteroids ahead for a millisecond. 'He knows we've got Stan and he's trying to stop us from crossing the Asteroid Belt.'

'Either that, or Hell is finally full.' Stan felt a horrible realisation dawn on him and he went cold with dread.

'Are those shapes dead people?'

'What else,' said Mercury. 'Hades has let loose the souls under his charge. Not all of them are Human, not all of them were ever really alive to begin with. Hades is not fussy when picking his armies.'

'And, sooner or later, they will lose their fear and they will attack,' added Mercury. 'For what have you to fear if you are already dead?'

Where was Mars? thought Stan anxiously. A second ago he felt cold, now he found he was sweating and his hands shook.

A wailing noise made him spin around. He shrank back in horror as everything bad or scary that had happened to him – ever – just faded away compared

to what he now saw. Seven hags scrabbled their way over the lip of a rock then propelled themselves forward on bony legs but at terrible speed, huge claws extending, long tongues flapping through cheekless mouths. Their bloodshot eyes were clearly visible to Stan – even from this distance – in contrast to the green flesh that hung from their bones like tattered rags.

'Turn!' he half shouted, half croaked at Venus, who managed to flick her huge wings in the confined space just in time to send out a jet of fire. Instantly the hags erupted in flames, their wails drowned out in the roaring furnace. Stan thought he was going to be sick as all seven of the terrifying creatures burst through the purple flames: blackened, the remnants of their hair on fire, eyeballs popping in the heat.

'Gnaargh!' was all Stan could manage, he had gone over the edge of fear into a whole new emotion. Gibbering, he reckoned. Just before the creatures reached them, Mercury sent off a concentrated pillar of fire that knocked the row of approaching hags sideways, their fire-brittle bones smashing against the cliff face of a larger asteroid.

More shapes appeared, crowding through the rock corridors around them: ghouls flapping their way through the vacuum; spirits with flowing death

shrouds flying in deadly convoys; spiny shapes like skeletal spiders hopped from asteroid to asteroid in a race to get to them.

'Nothing for it!' Mercury gasped, fire still leaking from his nostrils, 'We'll have to make a run for it.'

'Too late!' cried Venus as she sent out short bursts of flame in every direction, 'Our Auras can't break through the rock and they'll just cut us off and we'll be finished.'

Looking around, Stan could see she was right. 'What do we do?' he asked.

'*We* fight.' Mercury actually grinned. 'Not really my idea of fun, but it's what we do best, after all. You stay behind Venus, and try not to do anything heroic. Last thing you want is to die here, you'll end up like one of them,' he shuddered, 'with very bad breath.'

'But ...' although Stan was scared, it didn't seem right he should hide. He'd argued to be on this adventure after all, and felt responsible for all this, somehow. But before he could move forward, Venus shielded him with her wings.

'Stand aside, creatures of the dead!' she cried and blew a flat sheet of fire that shot out in a wave of flames ahead of them, like a deadly tide, 'or you will burn!'

But the ghouls showed no fear of the threat nor, indeed, any sign of having heard.

Hundreds now burst from holes in the rocks, the shadows and overhangs where they had been waiting to ambush Stan and his Dragon escort. They scuttled forward, jumping from boulder to boulder, bones clicking, lipless teeth grinning insanely, rusted swords and axes raking the air.

Venus and Mercury extended their necks to the full, whipping fire all around as Mars, who had been gaining height, finally joined the battle. He came in at supersonic speed, his own flames adding to the twisting infernoes: crimson, purple and silver. 'I've cleared a way through the rocks!' he shouted at the others, 'this is not his whole army, it's just a search party Hades sent. We just have to get rid of these and we're through.'

Stan's first battle, of a great many in his life, was short. But eventful, in the end. He had no doubt that had he not been safe inside Venus' Aura, he would have been burned to a stick of charcoal in seconds. The heat from the Dragons' furnaces lit up everything, making the floating boulders surrounding them glow red, then white hot as rank upon rank of the dead exploded into balls of fire and fell away, down into the inky, icy blackness below.

'Go back to the Realms of the Dead, from whence you came!' Venus roared.

'Ha, that'll learn yer!' Mars shot out red fireballs in every direction, which smashed the boulders and sent stone shrapnel into the oncoming hordes.

The battle was all but won now; Venus and Mercury doused their flames, leaving the survivors to Mars who flew after them, smashing their brittle bones with his powerful wings, racking them with his claws as he sent out narrow jets of flame like small missiles at the fleeing army. 'Ha ha! I haven't felt so good in centuries!' he cried.

'What a dear poppit,' Venus turned and flapped through the corridor in the boulders Mars had cut for them, 'I just knew he'd have a lovely time and he obviously hasn't been out, not properly, in such a while.'

'He'll sleep well tonight,' said Mercury.

They were passing a large rock the size of a floating island, but Venus and Mercury did not notice the last ghouls until it was too late. Scuttling out from where they lurked in a small cave, they made straight for Stan, as if sensing the weak spot. Venus tried to rear up to get out of range, but they were just too quick and they leapt at her, bursting through the Aura, right at Stan.

As if he'd been the target all along.

Before Stan could react, he realised he was sharing his safe bubble of Aura with three of the Undead. He smelled rotting flesh and saw fleshless hands with long yellow nails grasping for his throat. One carried a sword and had a manic look in its eye that, for some reason, made Stan think of Guy Murphy at the bus stop. Even out there, millions of miles away, the memory was still painful: it was the last time he

had been scared and hadn't known what to do. Just like now.

Fear was going to make him try to run away or stand there and do nothing. Just as he had done in front of Poppy at the bus stop, he was going to embarrass himself and these Dragons were going to see he was just a frightened little boy and they really were going to make him go home. In that split second as the ghouls tottered towards him, he also realised something else: everyone else on the adventure may have wanted this Particle of Light back, but that didn't mean they would save his sister as well. That was down to him.

He knew what he should do ... no, more than that, much more ... right *there* and *then*, Stan knew what he *had* to do.

Stan Pollux blinked once and lunged forward, grabbing the creature's rusting sword. It attempted to leap away, surprised that this smallish Human seemed to *actually* be attacking back, but Stan was too quick, he pulled hard and felt the brittle bones of his assailant come apart. Suddenly the sword was free. Stan swung blindly and the ghoul's head rolled off. That was pretty easy, he thought. He heard a sound, the clicking of dry bones and spun round, swinging the sword as he did so, taking another ghoul in the midriff, slicing it in half as it fell with a silent wail. Sensing a movement at his back, he turned again, the ancient sword raised above his head, and brought it down, crunching through bone and the rusting breastplate of some long dead warrior.

It was over in less than three seconds flat. Stan turned this way and that, looking for more creatures to fight, becoming slowly aware that there was a strange silence all around him. He stopped and looked up. The ghouls had gone and three Dragons were staring at him in stunned silence.

'Bloody hell, just who are you?' said Mercury under his breath.

'Doesn't talk much, but he can fight ... my kind of Human,' remarked Mars.

AGÔN

Pluto was the Roman god of death, who ruled the
underworld; his Greek name was Hades.
Pluto, the planet, is so far out in our solar system,
sunlight is the same intensity as moonlight on Earth.
Everything has an eerie glow ...

The black shadow that had been approaching for several minutes grew larger and more terrifying to Poppy the closer it came. She shrank back and held onto the crystal as tight as she could. Then the big shape landed with a loud crash on the stone floor and Poppy saw two huge wings open. Several jets of smoky flame shot out in lots of directions making twelve big fire bowls around the cavern burst into life. These gave off some light and also a lot of choking black fumes that hurt her already-sore throat.

This new creature was a Dragon, she recognised it from dozens of books on the shelf in her room and from lots of films.

Now she could see she'd been sitting on the cold stone floor of a huge building, like a church but with no roof, surrounded by night above. In the centre of the floor there was a great big scary hole and hundreds of staircases, all worn, all winding, twisting down into a huge cave. Deep within the cave, miles away, there now came a faint orange glow, like a volcano, as if the Dragon's arrival had woken it. Poppy coughed: the fires made scratchy smoke.

She thought about hiding, but she had absolutely no idea where. She took a deep breath and imagined what Stan would say. He'd be telling her she shouldn't be a cry baby, so she took another even deeper breath and stepped out of the shadows.

Dragons were big and could be dangerous, but in all those books and films, they were nearly always good. Most of the time.

This one didn't seem very nice, though. He looked like he was made of the black stuff that Daddy put on the barbeque to cook sausages, and he smelled all smoky. In a bad way. He also had great big wings, like a giant bat, which he tucked behind his back as he approached her, his eyes two red slits, windows to the glowing fire within.

In books, princesses and Dragons often went together: Poppy reminded herself of this as the Dragon crept closer, its head low, long neck extended. The smell of nasty things burning got stronger as the Dragon's lip curled back to show several rows of needle sharp teeth, many broken, all black. He seemed less like a Dragon, more like a snake.

'Soooo,' the Dragon's voice was a low hiss, 'the stars tell us of the return of demigods. My servants on Earth searched for you for years. The Fates are tricky with who they choose, so you were hard to find, well-hidden and just as well.' The creature smiled at Poppy in a way that didn't make her feel like smiling back. 'You hold the Particle of Light.'

Poppy frowned – what was he talking about?

As he trod around the massive hall, coal dust falling from his black scales he seemed uneasy. Cerberus, still in his corner, whined from three sets of dripping jaws. The black Dragon was pretending to be ignoring Poppy but he suddenly whipped his long neck around, his head coming close to her. She let out a little squeak of fear. The Dragon sucked air through his nostrils, like the twin exhausts of a lorry. 'Oh, yes, I smell it on her too Cerby.'

'Go away, bad Dragon!' Poppy could tell the monster was trying to scare her and that was unfair because she was still little and she was all alone.

She looked around for something that might protect her, but seeing nothing, she put her hand back in her pocket. Right then the crystal was the only thing that felt good. She didn't stop to think about why, the moment she touched it, she felt calmer; and she didn't ask herself, either, why she now brought the crystal out, holding it towards the Dragon who was staring at her with his scary, starey eyes and sharp teeth.

Poppy was surprised to see the Dragon flinch like their dog, Boris, when Mummy hit his nose with a magazine for chewing shoes. Something registered in her mind, something important: the Dragon seemed scared of her when she showed it Stan's rock from Granny.

The Dragon did his best to quickly hide his fear by raising himself up to his full height. 'I am Hades,' he boomed, 'Prince of the Darkness, Lord of the Dead … fear me or di—'

But Poppy stepped forward and the Dragon jumped back as if electrified. 'I said, fear me or you will perish!'

Poppy, feeling completely calm with the crystal in her hand, ignored it, stretched out and touched the Dragon with it. There was a flash and a smell of tar burning as Hades roared in pain and flew upwards in a panic, leathery wings flapping awkwardly.

Silence in the huge, echoing cavern.

Both girl and Dragon looked at each other for a long time: Poppy's bright, intelligent eyes assessing the situation on childish instinct, the Dragon watching through red, slitted eyes, millions of years old.

'Perhaps we got off on the wrong foot ...' Hades said eventually, his voice now like oil. 'I mean you no harm.

I have always loved your Earth ...'

'I want to go home now,' said Poppy.

'Sadly, I am trapped by the great father of Time, Chronos. Your Earth, that I once loved, is closed to me ... Cerberus here risked his life taking you, but more time near the crystal will destroy him.'

'But ...' Poppy was beginning to feel the first slight spasms of panic. She really, really wanted to go home.

'Patience, my princess,' Hades interrupted, 'the Particle of Light you hold, by right of your birth on Earth, has already started its important job, it has called those forces that will help me ... the Titans are made of our flesh and the Particle of Light will call them for revenge. They will finally finish their work they started a million generations ago. They will smash the Arch of Time and I will be free of this place!' He shot out a rolling plume of smoke and fire into the inky sky. Then he looked down, his voice quiet now, perfectly reasonable. 'You know we're very alike, you and I.'

Poppy thought of birthday parties, chocolate cake, nail varnish, ponies ... 'Do you like dressing up, too?'

'Um, what? No! I mean, yes of course I do! Who doesn't?'

Poppy narrowed her eyes, she could tell when grown ups were lying and this one was a very bad liar indeed.

The Dragon, who did not appear to notice her hard, distrusting stare, carried on.
'Oh, I have been watching you for weeks.

I understand you completely. We both know what it is like to be ignored, the youngest, the one who has to keep quiet and just do what they're told. The others laugh at us you know, take us for fools.'

Poppy said nothing but she did agree with that bit, the parts she understood, anyway.

'But in a little while our families will see us for who we are – for we will hold the power! You bear the Particle of Light, the key to all the great power in this Solar System, and I have the friends, shall we say, in dark places ... even now your brother is conspiring with our enemies, my spies have told him he is on his way to take the Particle of Light from you – take your power ... but he will have a surprise waiting for him! He is untested – he cannot possibly know his true power this soon ... and his friends are fools, they will never cross the River of Rock.'

Poppy stepped forward, making the Dragon stop. 'You're not going to hurt Stan, are you?' She had seen Stan disappear, and she wondered now where he was.

Pluto quickly realised he'd gone too far. 'Oh no no nnonnonno no ... I will not lay so much as a claw on him.' Poppy's eyes were drawn to the Dragon's feet and the huge claws that raked lumps out of the solid stone as he trod the great hall. 'But take it from one who knows, one who has spent over ten thousand years locked in the outer reaches of space, away from light, adrift in a cold, barren wasteland, that finally, after millennia, every-one ... and, yes, I mean everyone will get what they deserve!'

Poppy stared hard at the Dragon, who seemed very pleased with himself, although she couldn't think why. She was feeling better because she had learned something important in the last few minutes: she knew this Dragon and the big dog could not hurt her.

However, she did not know where her brother was and that was bad.

But, for now, she also knew when she had no choice but to wait.

JUPITER

Age: *6 million years*
Size: *149 tonnes*
Body made of: *Gas*
Fire: *Gold*

CHAPTER X

Jupiter is so gigantic that it is twice as big as all the other planets in the Solar System put together. The storm, which has raged across its surface for over three hundred years, is twice the size of Earth.

❄

NOTHING PREPARED STAN for the size of Jupiter. Up until now, 'big' was an idea he attached to elephants, family-sized packets of crisps in service stations, Mrs Pendar's bottom* ... and Australia.

Compared to all these things, compared to the other three planets Stan had visited recently, in fact, if Stan mentally piled up all the objects he had ever seen on one side and had Jupiter on the other, Jupiter would still make everything else look tiny.

The only thing that was larger was the Sun itself but, by now, it was so far away as to be barely a pinprick: a faintly more yellow dot than the other spots of light around their tired convoy. Out here, beyond the River of Rock, Space felt more pro-

* Year 3's classroom assistant.

found; a dark infinite silence, like a deep well of thoughts slowed by the vast gaps of nothingness between celestial bodies millions upon millions of miles apart.

There was no sign of Earth, and this gave Stan a pang of homesickness. He looked beyond the hugeness of Jupiter, out at the black on black depths of Deep Space and thought of Poppy out there somewhere. All on her own.

He decided to think about something else.

'You've shown yourself worthy to travel with us,

I am sorry I doubted you.' Venus had moved close to him.

'Um, thanks,' compliments at the best of times made Stan uncomfortable, but it seemed to be worse with Venus somehow.

If the colourful Dragon was aware he was embarrassed she did not show it. She turned and looked at him. 'Pluto did not send those ... creatures to stop *us*. He would have known we could have smashed our way through them. No, he had quite another target.'

'Who?' Stan had a feeling he wasn't going to like the answer.

'You, of course.'

'But ... why?' Stan was still confused about what

part he had to play in all this.

Venus shook her head. 'Pluto could always spot a threat. And sending his army that far from home shows he sees you as one. Perhaps Jupiter will know what to do with you and this missing girl with the Particle. Crossing the asteroids marks the line between the ancient Dragons and those of us who are younger. Jupiter, Neptune and Hades rule out here: the Air, the Seas and Underworld. Jupiter is the strongest but even he could be destroyed by the Particle of Light in the wrong hands in a blink of an eye. It is very powerful – we must get it back to where it belongs.'

'What about Uranus and Saturn?' Stan asked.

'They are very ancient! Uranus is the father of Saturn and Saturn the father of the three who rule now. Some say they sleep, some say they are imprisoned. But I have seen it prophesied in the heavens that they will come again.'

'Who put them in prison?'

'Their sons, of course – Jupiter, Neptune and Hades! How else could they rule?'

'But —'

'You are not of Dragon flesh or blood, perhaps you would not understand; although your emperors, your kings and kaisers have been just as ruthless, if

125

not worse. We are fire creatures after all and territorial. Our fire is the mark of our home planet, very like your knights' crests. It is as much part of us as our wings, our scales and our claws. It is the heart of each of us and it rules us: quicksilver for Mercury, rich purple is mine, of cobalt and acid ... the others? Well, Manchild, if you meet them you will see.'

The three Dragons now flew on in virtual silence, naturally taking a v-shape formation, with Mars at the arrowhead. Mars, who'd been very talkative after the short battle, became quieter the nearer they came the gas giant. Even Mercury stopped his chatter as they neared the Jovian Moons.

'That's Io, Europa, Ganymede, and Callisto,' murmured Venus, 'the guardians. They'll be our welcome party; officially no one is allowed to see the Great Dragon without their say so.'

Soon enough, Stan saw four shapes flapping towards them.

'I thought only planets had Dragons,' remarked Stan.

'No, there are some Moon Dragons left. But our numbers are dwindling, Stan – once there were more Dragons than you can possibly imagine, more than the stars in the sky. Your Earth was their

cradle: Dragons roamed your continents, flew through the air and swam in the deep seas, that is, until the first Titans struck.'

'You're talking about the dinosaurs?' asked Stan. 'They all died when a meteorite struck the Earth, except ...' He thought about it; stories got changed over time, he knew that. Maybe the meteorite was just another word for Titan or vice versa.

'Dinosaurs? They are gone and I have roamed far and not found another system where there are Dragons – either planet, moon or earth. But in Deep Space I have heard tell of dragons many times larger even than Jupiter. Some are made of huge clouds of fire and gas, light years across. It is said, they are travelling towards us and when they arrive, the Universe will end and a new one will be born of the fire that will consume the old.'

Before long, their welcome party drew level.

The Moon Dragons.

These were about a quarter of the size of the Planet Dragons. The other thing that made them different was the armour each wore. The lead Dragon had a bronze helmet that covered his face and bronze body plates, like large scales running down his sides. The others had similar protection but made from different materials: iron, silver and

possibly stone. With their shorter wings, they looked stocky, powerful and agile.

'Mercury the Messenger, Venus, errm, Mother and, if it isn't the great Mars ... welcome ... I guess. Now don't take this the wrong way but why in Hades are you here?'

'Push off squirts, or I'll flame grill you.' Mars looked like he was already trying to stop steam from coming out of his ears.

'We're here to see Dad, it's important, so just navigate us down, we're in a bit of a hurry, ta.' Mercury cut in.

'Sorry pal, no one gets to see the Boss these days. He's retired.'

'Look, we crossed the River of Rock and it nearly killed us. This is serious.' Mercury had gone from silver to grey to show his frustration.

'Oooh, sounds scary ... hmmm so let me think: you've come a long way, do I care? Let you guys down there or not ... um ... errr ... *thinking about it* ... Yep, got it! ... still no.'

'I'm warning you!' Mars looked like he was ready to unleash the torrent of fire at the smaller Dragons.

'Warn all you like, Mr. Tomato Face, you know you can't get through the storm down there without us

and if you fry me, you'll have Him to answer to. Read my fangs. We're Closed. No one Gets In. So, lovely to see you and all that. Go away.'

Up until now, Stan had been screened by Venus, but she had been waiting her moment, and just as it looked like Mars would turn into a fireball and engulf them all, she dipped her wings and the Moon Dragons saw Stan for the first time.

'Ah,' said the leading Moon Dragon in bronze armour, turning to stare at Stan. He let out a low whistle, 'Well, that changes things a bit. Why didn't you say you had one of *those* with you?'

'You didn't ask,' purred Venus.

'... and I take it he's not a normal one of Them.'

'He's got a temper on him. If you don't let us in, he'll probably have your head off ... take it from me, I've seen what he can do.' Mars growled.

'Easy, tiger,' the Moon Dragon turned to Stan, 'Wotcha, I'm Io. The Boss did say that if any of your lot turned up, especially one like, um ... you might be, then we had to bring him to you right away. He's been spending time in his observatory, looking deep into the Spiral Galaxy, says something big's going on with Earth and Humans. So, what's up with the Universe, Manchild?'

'Never you mind,' said Mercury, before Stan could

think of anything to say. 'Take us down, we haven't a moment to lose.'

'OK,' said Io, 'you know the drill, it's gonna get rough and just remember, you're only getting through because of the Manchild, so make sure he stays in one piece: bits have a habit of falling off Humans.' Stan looked to where Io was pointing and remembered the storm on Jupiter. The largest in the Solar System. They were so close now, and Jupiter filled Stan's field of vision: a huge tumbling mass of gas and, at its centre, like a planet within a planet, was the storm that raged through it. His dad had told him it had circled the planet for hundreds of years.

Whilst Stan hoped this was not their destination, at the same time he knew with a sinking heart it almost certainly was. He was beginning to realise that if there was a difficult and dangerous option, a Dragon would always go for that. Especially if it meant you'd probably end up terrified out of your wits and dead. However, the battle had given him some confidence – more than he'd felt in years, so he took a deep breath and promised himself he wouldn't close his eyes.

As they approached the dark spot revolving around the meridian of the gas giant, Stan felt the

winds buffeting them and saw the strain on the Dragons' wings as they were pushed this way and that, like giant airliners coming into land in bad weather.

As soon as they hit the outer reaches of the storm, a noise – like metal on metal – penetrated Venus' Aura and she was hurled sideways, crashing into Mars, as the other Dragons were scattered like leaves. Only the Moon Dragons, with their shorter, stronger wings seemed to stay on course.

'Sounds daft, I know, but we've got to head for the centre of the storm!' shouted Io over his shoulder. 'It's very important that you follow us closely, only we know the safe path through the turbulence! You go off limits it'll tear even you apart, Mars.' He was indicating a darker spot in the boiling cloud. Stan could see that the compact, more streamlined Moon Dragons were better suited to Jupiter's howling winds and realised, with a horrible sense of inevitability, they were heading towards the very eye of the storm.

Venus roared and turned herself with a huge effort, her wing membranes, like sails of a galleon, stretched to their full limit. They were heading in vaguely the right direction now but Stan, who felt like a pebble being shaken around a bottle, wasn't

sure they could hold their course for long. He glanced either side and could see that Mercury and Mars were having similar difficulties: Mars was using bursts of fire to keep his trajectory steady; and Mercury now tucked his wings away and went into an uncontrolled dive towards the eye.

By now the noise of the wind was deafening. Venus' Aura squeezed to nothing, so Stan felt himself being crushed. He gasped for air, trying his best not to pass out. Just as he was sure he couldn't take it any longer and that Venus' wings would surely snap under the strain; feeling buffeted, battered, and very seasick, they punched through the centre of the storm and suddenly found themselves in clear air.

The sudden calmness and peace was such a contrast to what they had endured just moments before, that Mercury started to laugh somewhat hysterically as the whole party swerved to a stop and hovered.

All around them, for thousands of miles up and down, the walls of the storm revolved, a dark orange cone of boiling cloud. It was like being in the eye of a hurricane ten thousand times deeper and more ferocious than on anything Earth. Far down below, floating in the midst of all this mayhem, a

great transparent castle slowly revolved, as if part of the giant merry-go-round.

Nothing had prepared Stan for this. 'What's it made of?' he asked, thinking that it looked like toughened glass or some kind of crystal.

'We call it Rhombus Rock, you call it diamond,' said Mercury shortly.

'The whole thing?' It was the most beautiful and probably the most expensive building in the Universe, Stan thought.

'It's the only thing that will withstand the storm,' said Mercury. 'Gods know why he can't live somewhere nice and quiet. I mean, Io's not bad – if you don't mind no atmosphere. And by that, I mean, it's boring and you can't breathe.'

'He doesn't like to be disturbed these days,' said the more serious Moon Dragon whom Mercury had said was Ganymede, as they landed by a huge diamond door that swung open at their approach. They started to walk through a silent hall. 'Hiding himself away,' Ganymede went on. 'I haven't seen him myself for over eight hundred cycles.'

'I think I saw him last week,' said another of their escort brightly.

'No you didn't, Cal,' Io turned to Stan and pointed a claw, 'that's Calisto, he spent the last decade hiding

in a hole – he's terrified of meteorite showers.'

'No I'm not!'

The fourth Moon Dragon suddenly spoke. 'West-bound on the A4 near Newbury a contraflow has been in place and traffic is slow between Junctions 9 and 10 on the M25. Today's weather is partly cloudy with some rain in the east ...'

'What's *he* talking about?' said Stan.

'Oh, don't listen to Europa, he's been broadcasting your news and weather channels since he swallowed one of your satellites.'

'It looked tasty!'

'It looked pointy.'

Stan was still feeling shaken from the descent into the eye of the great storm as they walked down a long corridor whose polished diamond walls rose up in vast colonnades and pillars with a faint blue tinge. It was silent in these halls and very hard to imagine the roaring winds outside.

'Who built this?' Stan knew that diamond was the hardest material that existed.

'Impressive eh? No one's got the faintest idea,' said Io, happy to be the tour guide. 'The Boss found it when he first settled here. He likes to make out it was for him, but Dragons are more your cave dwellers. This castle was here long before we arrived.

I've got a theory, though: it's a giant spaceship, made by aliens, those four big towers at the corners, are actually rocket boosters ... seriously, they could be,' he added when he saw the look on Stan's face, 'but whoever built it, they're long gone. When the Boss took over from his dad, he was looking for something in keeping, shall we say, with his new station in life – that is to say: big, impressive, freezing cold and expensive to run – so this is perfect!'

Mercury let out a low whistle. 'I've only heard about this.'

The corridor had come to an end at a pink-tinged arch and now it broadened out into a massive arena, like a huge roman amphitheatre. At the far end was a marble slab the size of a football pitch covered in parchments and papers, some of which had rolled onto the floor. Fussing over them was the largest Dragon Stan had ever seen in his, admittedly, brief acquaintance with the breed. However, the effect of *hugeness* was prevented from *greatness* by the fact the Dragon was wearing a very large knitted cardigan and what looked like bedroom slippers on two of its calloused feet.

'Did any of you know that squirrels on Earth can't burp or vomit?'

There was a long silence as the assembled company looked at the King of the gods and thought their own private thoughts.

'I did,' said Stan when it was clear no one else had anything to say.

The extremely large Dragon looked mildly surprised that someone had spoken at all. He looked this way and that, then peered at the group of Dragons in turn before coming to Stan.

'Clever boy,' he said, 'and who might you be?'

'I'm — '

'His name is Stan Pollux of Long Wittenham in Oxfordshire, Manchild, and ...' Mercury stepped forward, obviously keen to make sure he was fulfilling his Messenging Duties, '... Slayer of the Undead.' Stan liked the sound of that last bit. 'That one was just recently,' Mercury added.

The huge dragon peered at Stan and smiled. 'Absolutely delighted to meet you ... and I'm sure Mercury will get around to explaining the part about the Undead in his own good time. Oh, and hello the rest of you, excuse the attire, living in a diamond castle is as chilly and uncomfortable as any of you can imagine,' he turned to the Jovian Dragons, 'well done for keeping this boy in one piece, he and I are going to have to have a serious

talk later and Humans really are rather ... *breakable* ... and I find they're almost impossible to put back together.'

'Um, thank you, your Greatness.' Io looked a bit uncomfortable in the hall. 'Although this one here,' and he pointed at Mars, 'threatened to barbeque us if we didn't – against Union Rules an' that. He's not very nice.'

'Yes, I'm sure he did ... hello young Mars, been behaving yourself, I do hope?'

'Oh, hail, um, oh Mighty Lord of the Solar System, King of all, er, this stuff, and, um most places ...'

'Yes, yes, yes ... I'm very pleased you're here too, always nice to see one's children and I haven't heard from you in such a long time, even if Time in this dimension doesn't really exist before any of you *smarty pants* point that out to me.' He looked around again at them all and Stan noticed that in the last few minutes he'd seemed less old and bent, his eyes were brighter and he stared at them all with piercing intensity. 'Now, I don't mean to be rude, but why are you all here?'

Mercury stepped forward, looking nervous. 'Well, the Manchild saw Venus, I mean actually clapped his own eyes on her, even though she was hidden, or meant to be, and so she sent me back down to

Earth, to find out what's going on and I picked the boy up, took him to my cave and then we decided to go back to Earth and ...'

'Venus, perhaps you'd be so kind as to continue before we die of old age?'

Venus stepped forward and gave a sort of curtsey, looking almost girlish. She blushed, then looked serious. 'We've found the Particle of Light,' she said simply.

Jupiter raised a huge, horned eyebrow. 'Oh, good. Its location has been a worry and so you have it on you, or is that why you've got the boy, he's got it?'

'No.'

'As in no, he doesn't have it and nor do you?'

There was a very uncomfortable silence: Stan looked at his feet, everyone else, except Jupiter, looked at their claws. Eventually, Mercury cleared his throat. 'Hades might have it.'

'Ah, that's regrettable. Where was it for my brother to snatch such a prize?'

'It was in my rock collection, my granny gave it to me for my birthday, then my sister stole it.' Stan thought it was important to get his side of the story in early.

'Oh, well, that's sisters for you, I suppose,' Jupiter said, then stopped. He seemed to be thinking. 'How

did your family come to have it?'

Mercury, stepped forward again, looking like someone who was having a second chance to do their job. 'S'far as I can tell, the demigods have come back Earth. Stan may not look like much, but you haven't seen him fight. His sister has been captured by Cerberus, so we came here ... Hades, if he gets control over the Particle of Light, will use it to call the Titans back, as soon as they know it's discovered, they'll be back to destroy it.'

Jupiter remained silent for a bit. It seemed to Stan that the larger Dragon's thought processes were slower because of his size.

'Yes, this all sounds most serious and jolly worrying, I'm sure.' Jupiter studied the papers on his desk. 'Like some of you perhaps, I've been noticing new and surprising things in what the stars are saying, but nothing seems clear. Nevertheless, the Titans are powerful enough to take over running things. And it will not end well: our planets, including yours – the jewel of them all – will untether themselves from their orbits and float towards those beasts who will smash them to small lumps of rock. As you have all probably worked out, our only hope is to get the Particle of Light from Hades and return it to its rightful place. If we can

join it to the Sun, we may have a chance.' He peered at Stan from a great height, 'and you will be keen to find your sister, no doubt — '

'You'd have thought so, wouldn't you,' Mercury muttered under his breath.

' — but find her we must ... for the sake of our own Solar System!'

Stan watched as the Dragon shrugged off his cardigan and finally turned to face the others fully. It was then he saw that Jupiter, like his planet, was not solid at all, instead he was gas in the form of a Dragon. Without his cardigan, he was virtually transparent. Flame-coloured fumes billowed around his edges, like a fiery halo, and Stan saw that all traces of an elderly old man fussing over books had gone: up until then he'd reminded him of Mr. Stevens, their headmaster, but now Stan felt a little afraid of him. Jupiter rose up to his full height and looked down on them all.

'We must to war!' he boomed.

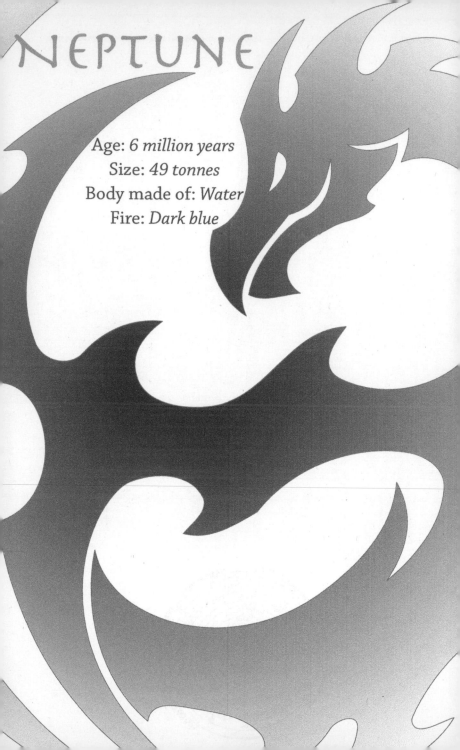

NEPTUNE

Age: *6 million years*
Size: *49 tonnes*
Body made of: *Water*
Fire: *Dark blue*

CHAPTER XI

Jupiter, whose other name is Jove,
has his sacred day of the week on a Thursday,
which is the special day of another king of the gods –
Thor, the 'Viking' god.

❄

STAN WAS INVITED TO REST before supper, and Io showed him to some smaller apartments off the main trunk of the castle. They were smaller, almost Human-sized, surprisingly well furnished and comfortable. Up until then, Stan hadn't realised how tired he was, but the minute he lay down on the huge quilted bed, he fell fast asleep and dreamed he was back in Long Wittenham; in his room, playing on his computer. It was a comforting sort of dream but then it changed and he was once again riding on the back of a huge, unfamiliar Dragon, a sword in his hands and flames everywhere he looked. He tilted the sword towards a bright star that had a black dot at its centre, the Dragon sent out a fire

corridor and they raced towards the star at light speed. The black hole became larger and ... Stan opened his eyes.

His heart was racing. He lay there for a while, keeping very still, forcing his breathing to slow. By and by it did, and he started wondering about Poppy again, where she was and whether she was in such terrible danger. It felt sort of weird to be worried about her, like it was not really his job, but neither his mum or dad was there to do it, so he guessed it was down to him.

There was a bang on the door. It was Io. 'Wakey wakey, we're to have a feast tonight, first time the family have been together in ten thousand years, calls for some sort of celebration, I'd say.'

'OK.'

As they walked along Io seemed quite cheerful. 'More going on down here than in centuries: Neptune has turned up and Saturn is on his way.'

'What about Uranus?'

'He doesn't really like being called that. I'm sure you can guess why?' Io grinned hopefully.

'OK, I won't call him that then,' said Stan, completely straight-faced.

'Right, well,' Io looked a bit put out. 'Silent type.'

Stan was spared having to answer that as they

turned into a corridor that sloped towards a huge glittering hall: a long table of black marble stood out against the polished diamond surfaces, and there were nine thrones in all, although only seven had Dragons sitting in them. Io, who was evidently pleased at the effect on Stan, explained the seating as they walked down the hall under the gaze of seven huge creatures.

'So, Jupiter sits at the head, his throne is diamond. His brothers: Neptune on blue emerald, Hades would be on the black onyx, beside him and then his children: Mars on a ruby throne, bit gaudy if you ask me, Venus pearl, and Mercury, silver. At the end, Granddad – Chronos or Saturn, some call him, and then the oldest of them all, Caelus would normally sit.'

'Caelus?'

'Yeah, you know,' Io wiggled his eyebrows, 'Ur ...'

'Caelus sleeps, some say he will wake only when he is needed. The Father of Time will be there when Time in your dimension finally runs out.' Venus smiled down at the pair of them.

'Oh,' this seemed important to Stan, 'when's that?'

'No-one but Caelus knows.' Io walked on with Stan. 'I personally don't think it's going to happen for a bit, so don't worry. Saturn created the Arch of Time not

just for you, but to trap his brother Hades, and stop him causing any more mischief ... not that that's worked.'

Stan gaped at the huge braziers of fire that had been lit behind each Dragon, showing their respective fires: red for Mars, silver for Mercury, purple for Venus. Jupiter's was the colour of the Sun just before it sets: a rich, molten gold. Neptune's was blue, like the Dragon himself, wavy and liquid. Stan stared at the new arrival, knowing it was rude, but unable to take his eyes off him. The huge aquamarine Dragon bowed his ancient head gravely as Stan filed past, ripples like oil on water spreading across his scales. Stan gave a sort of awkward wave, then felt ridiculous. What was he, five? Who *waved* at a Dragon?

'Welcome, boy known as Stan!' Jupiter seemed much younger – even fiercer – than before. His eyes positively twinkled. 'This is an important evening – you, young man, will represent the ninth planet in the first dimension, no Human has sat on this council since the Demigods. Perhaps indeed you are one of them. Come sit beside me and we will try to find out together.'

At that, Hades' onyx throne was removed by Jovian Moon Dragons Ganymede and Callisto, and

a smaller seat, tall enough to reach the high table but propped up with rich velvet cushions and gold inlaid rugs was put in its place. Earth's throne was a swirling mix of blue, green and white stone, the colour of his planet, and looking at it made Stan feel homesick all over again.

'I trust your throne is to your liking, young man?'

'Uh huh,' Stan nodded and blinked several times. Jupiter, who seemed not to notice his embarrassment, flapped his huge wings open, each tip reaching right across the great banqueting hall.

'Welcome, we have been apart for too long, we who represent the elements, the very fabric of the Solar System ... and all its faults, too, lest we get big for our boots. It is a pity we are united again for war but I feel glad in my heart to see you all. Without further delay, let the feast begin!'

And a stranger meal Stan had never seen.

For the first course, each Dragon had a cauldron of dark larva placed before them that burned Stan's eyes just to look at. They drank deep, without a word, the flowing fire blazing within their scaled throats and stomachs as they swallowed the searing liquid.

The solemn part over, they all became quite chatty with one another as more platters, cauldrons

and crucibles were brought in by the Moon Dragons. There were soups of gases: hydrochloric acid, argon and glowing neon that they sucked up through their nostrils and exhaled with sighs of tremendous pleasure; there were jellied crystals on beds of ice surrounded by liquid nitrogen – ruby, amethyst, malachite; huge bunches of pearls were consumed like grapes between courses; a craggy dish, like a small mountain, was lowered from the ceiling. 'My favourite!' exclaimed Jupiter, highly delighted, 'Extremely rare radon harvested from a supernova light years from here, topped with cobalt. I would let you try some, my dear boy, but it would melt your intestines – and we can't have that! Try this instead?'

Stan took a bite from a small plate in front of him piled with slices of white meat. 'It tastes just like roast chicken!' he exclaimed.

Jupiter looked very pleased. 'Dragons have a complicated internal chemistry, we make fire, but if nothing else we understand the ingredients of the universe. We live amongst the base elements. Your planet is the perfect mix of these. If you've got the right chemicals, you can make anything – even that chicken.'

Just as he finished speaking, there was a com-

motion at the end of the hall and Stan saw the final guest arrive.

It was obvious to Stan immediately who this was. 'I know, that's Saturn!' he blurted out a bit too loudly, causing the new arrival to turn and glare at him. Saturn, like Jupiter, was made entirely of gas, yet his was spread thin, so that he seemed to swirl at the edges as he trod the length of the hall. And all about him rocks representing his many moons twisted and turned. Stan knew there were over one hundred and fifty. He struggled to remember some of their names: Pandora, Prometheus, Janus ... the effect of the moons was like the rings of the planet itself around the silent, brooding Dragon.

Saturn was sombre, with none of the humour the others had, and he regarded the rest in angry silence.

'Welcome, father!' boomed Jupiter, the only one around the table who seemed unaware the happy atmosphere had just flooded out of the room – as if someone had left a door open on a cold night. Saturn glared about him and everyone else shifted uncomfortably on their thrones. 'Sit and feast with us, we've just got to the best bit in fact. I think it's your favourite, too. Cersei Nebular Blancmange, it's out-of-this-world. Ha ha!'

'Damn your feast, and may your fires die and your wings crumble.'

'Nice to see you too!' muttered Mercury.

'What's that?!' the very old Dragon glared about him, his gases swirling angrily.

'He meant nothing, Grandfather,' Venus tried to smile but she was looking tense.

'I did, too – I meant, why are you here?' Mercury looked tense too, his scales had gone dark grey.

'Uh oh,' said Io, from behind a large urn.

Saturn billowed red and reared up on his hind legs, 'You dare question me, you pipsqueak ... you, you ... *lizard*!'

'Calm down, father, and have some pudding,' Jupiter was the only Dragon who seemed relaxed.

'Calm down? You great ball of hot air – you steal my crown, then you summon me like a common Moon Dragon!'

'Charming,' Io's tail could be seen flicking behind the pot. Jupiter's great brow furrowed.

'I can see that it was a mistake to ask you to come, so you may go,'

'Brother,' Neptune half rose, 'our father deserves more respect.'

'He doesn't even deserve a place at this table!' Mars cried.

'Or pudding.'

'Shut up!' several Dragons turned on Io.

'Yeah!' Mercury glared at Io, then at Saturn, 'We risked our lives to get here ...'

Venus turned to him. 'Shh, brother, this is not our fight.'

'Everything's my fight.' Mars wasn't going to be left out.

'Leave, Father!' said Jupiter, now deadly serious.

'You no longer rule the firmament, you have hidden down here in this ridiculous alien hovel for too long ...'

'Risked your lives ... just crossing a few rocks?'

' ... war is not the only answer to everything.'

' ... when did you last leave your armchair, Grandad?'

Stan listened, as the room erupted into mini arguments that flew across the table like angry wasps. He was feeling more and more like he did when his parents fought. It was always over something a bit pointless, just like now, and the squabbling never solved anything, *just like now*.

Stan couldn't understand why they thought that shouting louder than the person next to them would help. There was too much talking both here and on Earth, as far as he was concerned.

Normally, during arguments, he and Poppy kept quiet until his parents stopped and he supposed he should just stay out of it, but ... he imagined what was going on at home right now: his mum discovering they were gone and calling his dad, then the police and then his granny, who would be beside herself. Then Stan thought of Poppy – Pluto was so far away from the rest of the planets it wasn't even a planet, just a rock of ice adrift in millions of miles of space ... Stan felt a surge of anger, like he had when he had taken hold of the sword in the battle. He looked around the room: Neptune was shooting blue fire across the ceiling, roaring about someone chopping the head off his favourite Hydra; Mars was throwing plates of food ... and everyone else was shouting and no-one cared about what was really important and he had just fought off a pack of ghouls without anyone's help, so he deserved to be treated like a grown-up and when he thought about it, he was acting more grown up than any of them put together ... just then, something that looked like a ball of ice flew across the table, hurled at Mars by Neptune ... Without another thought, Stan grabbed a knife and sliced through the missile in one clean sweep, sending crystals in a shower of ice across the whole table. 'BEEEE QUIEEET!!!!' he roared, with

more energy and authority than anything he had uttered in his whole life.

Everyone stopped.

There was dead silence.

All the Dragons slowly turned, their scales creaking, and looked at Stan through million-year-old eyes ... creatures with jaws like caves full of razors.

But Stan glared back, too angry to wonder if a Dragon was about to burn him to a crisp or bite his head off. The knife was still in his hand, so he slammed the point deep into the table. He felt words tumble into his brain, and instead of getting stuck there, for the first time in his life, they started to come out of his mouth.

'You're all acting like idiots ... no wonder we stopped worshipping you, you're not gods you're just big babies. You say the Solar System is in danger right now, but you're more worried about things that happened ten thousand years ago that no one remembers, or even they do, it's just stories. I'm the only one here who wants to save the Solar System, because ...' Stan paused, but just for a moment, as he'd not said as many words for any reason in his life, but he didn't feel like stopping just yet, '... I want to save the Solar System because it's where I live, it's where I go to school, it's got my mum and

153

dad in it, the dog and ... and it's got my sister – and I've got to get her back and you have to help me because you said you would and you let me come along and that's all about Taking Responsibility for your Actions, and even I know that and I'm only eleven which is 1,999,989 years less than you, so you need to sort yourselves out ... right now!'

There was another long silence as he sat back down. The knife, stuck in the table, was still vibrating faintly.

'I like this Human,' said Saturn.

'Reminds me of Old Hercules, but his table manners are better,' added Jupiter.

'And he's right,' added Venus.

❄

Half an hour later, the Moon Dragons had cleared up the mess and Jupiter turned to them all. 'We are ever fools whilst the Solar System is in terrible danger. We must put our petty fights behind us to protect our own worlds but also the jewel – Eden – Earth! For although Men have forgotten us, it is clear the strength of heroes still walks amongst them, even if they are just eleven years old and go to school!' He smiled at Stan, who went red.

'Well done, Stan,' whispered Mercury. 'The shortest council I've ever been to, they normally last for years before anyone agrees about anything.'

'So to war it is!' cried Saturn. 'Eight sacred planets allied against the forces of darkness.'

'This just gets better and better.' Mars was positively glowing.

Saturn turned to Stan. 'Mars was telling me about your fearlessness and skill with a sword.' Stan, who was still very uncomfortable with all this talk said absolutely nothing. 'Well, if we are going to war, then I have a gift for you!'

Io came over, dragging a gold casket. 'His nibs brought this along, looks important.' He flicked the lid open. 'Ta da!' he said.

Stan peered inside, his eyes widening at what he saw. 'It's armour?'

'This suit was made for Apollo to explore between the planets and fly about the Sun, though you'd have to ask him why that was so important – there's really nothing there ... just a lot of hydrogen ... on fire. He probably did it just to show off ... that was Apollo all over. With this suit, he would not need a Dragon's Aura to protect him. Very convenient – it also meant he could get up to all sorts of mischief no one had thought of before they let him go

charging about the cosmos in a suit that made him nearly invincible.' The very old Dragon glared at Stan. 'We're not going to have any nonsense from you, are we?'

Stan peered at the shining gold metal breastplate, inlaid with intricate carving that looked like a map of the stars. When he looked closer, he could see their solar system with the Sun and all the planets, then further out all the solar systems of the Milky Way. It was amazing. 'How was it made?'

'Wayland, smith to the gods, fashioned it from metal mined from a deep space meteorite – light as graphite, more resistant than diamond, impervious to heat, cold and radiation, probably had air con.'

'Can I ...?'

'Yes, yes – I'm giving it to you!'

Stan had meant could he touch it, not own it. He couldn't quite believe his eyes (or his ears) and so he just stood there stupidly, staring at the onyx casket with its clear diamond screen drawn back. Something occurred to him. 'Won't it be too big?'

Saturn treated him to a slow smile, although, like all Dragons – Stan was beginning to realise – this was always a bit alarming ... as in it looked a little like they were preparing to eat you.

'No, the Febus Armour will mould itself to the

wearer. It needs to be a perfect fit, not so much as a hairline crack between you and Space or you'll freeze in seconds – that is Wayland's genius. It also means anyone who pinches it can ride off into the sunset and give us all a headache. So, don't leave it just lying about, I know what small boys are like.'

Next to the armour lay a sword. Saturn saw where Stan's eye travelled. 'Yes, it's a big sharp sword – and another good reason, I've kept this suit under my personal supervision for the last few millennia. I did ask Wayland not to make it – too risky I said, give him some protection, happy to do that for the boy but don't arm him. But, oh no, I was just Head of the Gods in those days and the most powerful creature you'll meet this side of the Galaxy, can't think why you'd listen to me. So, Wayland went ahead anyway, when I wasn't looking, and made the sword from rhodium, one of the brightest and rarest metals in the universe. Just as well, far too expensive, I thought, to be any use, when I did find out what that nincompoop did behind my back – just a sort of ceremonial thing. Then young Apollo only goes and lops off the giant, Tityus', head with it. One swipe and a noggin the size of a small house was rolling across the carpet. Caused no end of trouble that did but does show that Wayland knew

157

what he was about, I suppose, when it comes to making sharp swords. Anyway, you'll be needing all that where you're going,' the Dragon waved a claw airily in the direction of the armour, as if he'd already lost interest, 'so you'd best try it all on, make sure it hasn't sprung a leak or anything.'

'Really?'

'No, I was joking, first sign of any more trouble, we mean to throw you into Space – see if your head explodes before your blood freezes or your brain comes out your ears first ... it'll be *funny* ... it'll take our minds off being attacked by angry Titans.'

'Don't listen to him,' purred Venus, coming between them. She gave Saturn a mock stern look. 'He's been grumpy ever since the fall of the Roman Empire. The Febus Armour is yours now,' then she turned away and looked into the distance. Stan knew that look well enough, his mother did it when she didn't want people to know what she was thinking. 'I'm sure you won't need it,' but there was concern in her voice nonetheless.

Unable to contain himself any more, Stan ran forward and picked up the breastplate, surprised at how light it felt. He went to pull it over his head.

'Nah,' said Mercury, coming over with a big grin, 'clothes off, or it'll not fit right.'

'What?' Stan felt his world slip sideways. He hadn't taken his clothes off in front of anyone since he was about six, and he certainly didn't feel like doing it in front of this lot. They were scary enough as it was. Plus there was that issue of the pants that had just occurred to him.

'Um ...' invincible armour or not, this was a deal breaker.

'Don't worry, my poor darling, I'll shield you,' said Venus coming to his rescue. Again. And, with that, she spread her scarlet and green wings.

Within a few minutes, Stan had got his clothes off and the suit on. If he'd been worried he would not know how it fitted together, he needn't have been. The suit seemed to do all that for him. Once he got the breastplate over his head, he reached for the arms and they slotted into place as if pulled by magnets. The same with the gloves, which had metal backing for protection, but some kind of leather on the palms, thick but soft and supple, so his hands moved without the clumsy ski-glove feeling. They clipped into the arms and Stan felt the seal tighten around the join. The only thing that had been tricky was strapping the sword on, but that came last and by then he was fully clothed and he no longer felt embarrassed, just ecstatic.

'And tidy up that pile of clothes,' snapped Jupiter, lumbering over. 'By the gods, I've forgotten how messy young Human males are.'

'Sorry,' said Stan and he made a half-hearted attempt to kick the various messy piles of clothes into one slightly neater pile. Saturn sighed and let out a narrow jet of very hot flame. 'There,' he said with some satisfaction, wandering off again, 'seems I have to do everything around here.'

Stan was still staring at the smoking pile of ash that had been his clothes when Venus came over. 'Nice armour,' she said. Then, coming up very close, added, 'Who's *Ben Ten*?'

SATURN

Age: *7.5 million years*
Size: *113 tonnes*
Body made of: *Gas*
Fire: *Bronze*

CHAPTER XII

Saturn was the Roman god of time.
His name was Chronos in Greek.
The Saturnian planet rings are made
mostly of chunks of ice.
The rings stretch out more than 120,700 km
from the planet, but are amazingly thin:
only about 20 metres thick.

❄

IN SPITE OF HIS NAP EARLIER, Stan was certain he would stay awake until it was time to go. However, he surprised himself by falling fast asleep almost immediately.

He had no idea how long he slept but, when he woke, he felt relaxed and deliciously rested, which was strange – considering there was a very good chance that he was going into battle that day. Just before they had left the great hall, Jupiter had asked to look at Stan's hands under Saturn's watchful gaze. Both the terrible old Dragons had stared at the lines

on the palm of his hands in silence for a long time. 'What say you father?' Jupiter had asked quietly.

'I say he's your problem, I'm retired!' And with that the ancient Dragon swept out of the room, his rings swirling about his body. 'I'm still coming if there's going to be any fighting,' he barked over his shoulder.

❄

Stan was coming out of the bathroom, when Io barged in. 'Did you wash you hands?'

'Er ...' Stan went back in and came out about thirty seconds later.

'Cleanliness is next to godliness, as we say around here,' said Io.

'Mum says it too,' mumbled Stan.

'She probably says don't forget to make your bed, also.'

❄

The gathered Dragons looked up at the eye of the storm. It was even more impressive in the dawn of Jupiter. Blue and orange light filtered through the vast, silent whirlpool all around them, towering

over ten thousand miles high, swirling at speeds Stan could barely comprehend.

'I never get used to it,' Io stood next to him.

'How does the castle stay right in the middle?'

'Beats me. Asked the Boss that once and he got a bit shirty. Don't think he really understands it either, but you can't admit not knowing something if you're King of the gods.'

In silence, the Dragons made themselves ready. Io and the other Jovians went over and grouped themselves around Jupiter, like a protective guard. Venus came and stood next to Stan on one side, Mercury on the other.

'You will not require my Aura, now you have the Febus Armour.'

'Ho, hum, they grow up so fast,' sighed Mercury. 'Don't worry, we'll stick close. Mind you, after your last performance, I'd say it was more for other people's safety, not yours. Reminds me what Jason once said about a group of goats who tried to eat his fleece, actually it's a very funny story —'

'It is time!' Jupiter cut in and shot out a rich gold flame as he took to the air. For such a large and ancient beast, his flight was surprisingly agile. Up he spiralled through the vortex in the eye of the storm; the Moon Dragons, then Neptune, Uranus, Mars,

Venus and Mercury following hard behind them, rising on the thermal currents, almost like seagulls Stan had seen on holiday.

Here goes, thought Stan. Up until now, he had no idea how the armour would actually work, but Mercury had explained he needed only to think where he wanted to go and the suit would do the rest. Sure enough, when Stan put the visor of the helm down and thought up he shot towards the gracefully circling Dragons. Stop! He thought urgently, as his armour took him narrowly past Mercury's silver wing tip and bumped roughly against Mars' Aura. This was a mistake, as it seemed stop also meant the armour lost flight, and Stan found himself falling back to the castle far below. *Stooop!* he thought frantically, no that doesn't work ... *Wait?* ... Nothing happened and he was now only a few thousand feet from the polished diamond surface of the courtyard. Hitting that was going to hurt, armour or not. *Hover*, he thought, and he halted in the air, bobbing up and down. Phew! OK, I just need to concentrate my thoughts, be more precise. Follow the Dragons, he commanded the suit and this time he rose up more gracefully.

No-one could remember the last time so many Planet Dragons were gathered in full flight, but the

need had never been greater. The formation was truly magnificent, had there been anything other than the cold cosmos and a few passing hunks of comet ice to see them. They passed by another huge planet – an ice giant. Stan gasped in wonder as they arched away from its pale blue surface, the Dragons silent. In reverence.

'That's where Uranus sleeps, he's the grandfather of Jupiter, Hades and Neptune, father to Saturn,' said Mercury to Stan. 'It would break his heart to see how they fight, but he was pretty feisty in his day. Seems we've always been at war. If we've got no one to fight, we'll fight amongst ourselves. Just as well you stopped worshipping us, we had to take things a bit quieter after that.'

EPISODE 11

The big black Dragon reminded Poppy of Daddy when he was waiting ages for Mummy to get ready to go out.

He was stamping up and down the hall impatiently. It was freezing, the whole planet seemed to be a big ball of ice and it was not surprising that Poppy could see her breath billowing like that of a small Dragon, each time she breathed. She shivered. Down below, fires burned in contrast to the permafrost above. Looking at their glow made her shiver, too. But in a different way.

'It is nearly time,' Hades said under his breath. 'The Titans heed the call of the Particle of Light and they will come. I will give them the Particle and in gratitude, they will destroy the Arch of Time, cast down Jupiter, his fawning friends and the rest of my cruel family. I will have my revenge and my freedom! Then the dead will rise to rule the living!'

Poppy remained in the shadows, the crystal in her small, hot hand. For all his stamping about, she could see Hades was worried. Cerberus, the large dog, could sense it, too. He was quiet in his corner, occasionally pawing the ground and sniffing the air.

It was funny: on Earth the crystal had been pretty but not really that special. Way out here it was larger in her hand, and gave off a comforting glow that seeped into her body and warmed her through. It also seemed to react to her and when she held it up the Particle of Light glowed with a golden fire, deep within its facets.

It was all she had, but was perhaps just what she needed.

'It reacts to you,' Hades had stopped his pacing and was watching her closely. 'The Particle of Light wasn't handed to you by chance, it came to you. I think it chose its mistress. Oh, I see that now.' He stepped closer making Poppy step back. She held the Particle of Light up protectively and Hades halted, but this time a smile played on his sharp, draconian features. 'Oh, if only you knew the power you could wield with that thing.'

'Go away,' Poppy had no idea what the big monster was getting at but enough adults in her short life had tried to get her to do things she had no intention of doing and she had a pretty good idea that this was one of those times. Even if the adult in question was a two tonne Dragon made of black smoke and frozen flesh.

'As I was saying, you and I have more in common than you think. We could be a good team – the underdogs rising up. Our parents think so little of us and our own brothers pour scorn on everything we do.' Hades smiled nonchalantly as Poppy raised the crystal higher. He seemed more confident now, thé Girlchild did not really mean to harm him, she was scared and what she needed most was a friend – he would be that friend!

And then he would control her.

Perhaps they would not need the Titans after all? He stepped forward, Humans were basically weak and this one was all alone and so small, he'd scare her and then ... he stopped as a rock bounced off the end of his nose ... he glared at the small girl who glared back. Now you die! Hades took a deep breath, sucking in fire to burn this pipsqueak to a cinder but then there was another blinding flash as he was thrown backwards, sliding across the floor, smashing through pillars, buttresses, and finally coming to a standstill when his head slammed against the central colonnade. Hades stared in disbelief across the hall at the evil little tyke, thinking a thousand murderous thoughts backed up by a million years of experience punishing the dead.

About fifty yards away, Poppy sat down on a stone bench, her legs swinging, and smiled at him sweetly.

'Good Dragon now,' she said, the crystal glowing warmly in her small hand.

PLUTO
Age: *6 million years*
Size: *2 tonnes*
Body made of: *Charcoal,
clinker and onyx*
Fire: *Soot-black*

CHAPTER XIII

The Styx, one of Pluto's moons,
takes its name from the river dead souls
needed to cross to get to the Underworld.

❄

HADES WAS JUST ABOUT TO EXPLAIN how the minute she no longer had the Particle of Light, he was going to cook and eat Poppy in one fiery gulp, when he stopped.

His black scales went a sort of sickly grey.

'Cerby?' The three-headed dog looked up. 'You weren't followed were you?'

Cerberus looked down quickly and frowned at its paws, trying not to meet its master's level gaze.

'Well, whatever, they're coming – I can feel them.'

Poppy looked up, whoever it was on their way, Hades was now looking scared. 'Is Stan nearly here?'

Pluto ignored her, seemingly speaking to himself. 'What? That's not possible. No.'

'He is?' Poppy felt a burst of hope in her chest.

'And the rest of them! My brothers, the others. *Dragons!* They must have destroyed the vanguard I sent out to the River of Rocks, otherwise I would have been warned. Cerberus! Damn the Styx, open the gates of the Underworld. It is time to release the Legions of the Dead! We will meet them in battle at the Arch of Time!'

❄

Dragons rely on sense of smell and telepathy as much as sight. But it was Stan who saw the cloud coming first.

They had long since passed Neptune's deep blue planet and were flying into Deep Space, surrounded by blackness. Slowly a pinprick of light appeared that Stan supposed was Pluto, and his stomach gave a small somersault.

As the dwarf planet grew in size, Stan saw a flat cloud, like a shroud – and he knew, in his heart, that once whatever was in the cloud got to them, there would be no going back.

This was it.

Up until then, he'd been enjoying so much the amazing sense of being able to fly through Space

he'd almost forgotten why they were in convoy. Flying at roughly the speed of a comet without bits falling off is a good way to keep your mind off having to fight a zombie army, in a vacuum over three billion miles from home ... the suit was incredible, but now he'd need to find out how well it stood up in battle ... he also needed to find out how well *he* stood up in battle – if he was really brave after all, or if what had happened at the River of Rock had been a fluke.

Jupiter reared up and let out a burst of golden flame. 'Hades sensed us coming, he has released his Horde!'

'Oh goody, just what I love, more dead people,' said Mercury.

Mars banked back and pulled level with Stan. 'It would be an honour if you were to ride with me into battle!' he barked.

'Er, OK,' said Stan, experiencing the twin emotions of being pleased someone else would be driving as he hadn't quite got the hang of the suit yet, and nervous that Mars would definitely be leading him into the thick of the fight.

He thrust his heels down, feeling the armoured suit slow, and Mars drew alongside, allowing Stan to grab a wing and swing himself over the Dragon's

back so he was sitting where Mars' long neck joined his shoulders. It was surprisingly comfortable.

'Just be careful when you draw that sword of yours not to chop my wings off. It was forged in the fires of my great Volcano, Olympus Mons and it will cut through even my scales.'

Stan drew the sword for the first time and gave it a couple of practice swipes. It was better balanced than the sword he had pulled from the ghoul's bony hand. It felt like an extension of his arm and moved through the airless atmosphere like light. 'Don't worry,' he said, surprised at the confidence in his voice and how natural the sword felt in his hands, 'I know what I'm doing.'

'I think you do,' said Mars. 'So, demigod, are you ready to fight?'

'Yes,' said Stan. And he actually meant it.

Poppy shrank against the walls and hid her small face in fear: tens of thousands of screaming souls poured from the depths below, like a swarm of ragged bats.

The first wave of Hades' army was the horsed cavalry of the dead. Ancient knights riding skeleton

horses galloped across the black, frozen sky to meet the Dragons at the Arch of Time – a huge bridge of ice spanning the dark side of the planet Pluto, like the giant buttress of a cathedral.

Just ten thousand miles away, sensing how close to his sister he was – virtually next door, in space terms – Stan watched them coming. He was gripping his sword so tightly his fingers hurt.

The dead knights' armour was impressive until they got close and Stan saw it was full of holes and gashes, evidence of how they had met their end on Earth. They carried spears and lances, and mixed in with their medieval ranks were other mounted troops from different times and places: Egyptian horsemen, Mongols and Saracens in light armour, holding long, curved swords in bony fingers.

Stan was glad that most wore helmets with visors, for the few that didn't grinned back at him through lipless mouths, as if the whole thing was one huge joke. Stan felt real fear now, but Mars sent out a concentrated blast of molten red fire and the front ranks coming towards them evaporated in flame and ash. They can be beaten, Stan thought, and he felt his fear give way to excitement.

'GLOOORRRRYYYY AND HONNNOOUURRRR!' bellowed Mars, laughing and flying straight into

their ranks, smashing through metal and bone, breaking lance and sword in one great sweep of his wings.

A few of the phantom knights tried to come around the back of Mars, but Stan was ready for them. The sword flashed in his hand, feeling astonishingly smooth as it cut through their armour, and the dry bodies within exploded into clouds of dust. One knight thrust a rusty lance at Stan, it went under his guard and scraped along his armour. Stan grabbed the lance and pulled and, as the deathly horseman leaned forward, Stan brought the blade of his sword straight down and his opponent's bones shattered into hundreds of jagged shards.

They were through the first wave of cavalry now and Mars banked sharply. Stan could see that the rest of the Dragons were all fighting hard. Venus and Mercury had followed them and were pounding the left and right flanks with their iron-hard claws. Below them, Stan saw Jupiter launch his own attack on a fleet of ghost ships that swept from the dark reaches behind Pluto's moon of Styx. The ships had all sunk or been destroyed and Stan could see the stars and Pluto's other Moons of Charon, Nix, Kerberos, and Hydra through holes in a

thousand phantom keels.

Jupiter, all traces of the kindly old Dragon gone, sent out rivers of bright gold flame that swept into the galleons with their torn sails and tattered masts. The fleet was so tightly packed that as one broken ship caught light, it spread like wildfire across to others, so soon Hades' fleet burned red across the dark skies. Jupiter's Moon Dragons fought the zombie marines as they tried to jump from ships and escape the flames.

'Once more into the fray!' Mars roared and banked, shooting into the cavalry that was in now in total panic. He had never been much good at anything before: lessons, football or even making friends but Stan, the sword spinning in his hands, sliced left and right. He had finally found something that he was good at. Extremely good.

Slowly a bubble formed around the red Dragon and its rider. The rearguard of Hades' army feared them both and held back. 'Come on and fight us!' shouted Mars, 'what have you got to be afraid of, you're already dead!'

'This is easy!' shouted Stan. Hades' whole army had stopped in its tracks and the Dragons were smashing great holes in their ranks with fire and claw and sword. The battle, it seemed, would soon

be over.

But he had spoken too soon.

✳

Saturn broke away from the remnants of a small battalion of Roman chariots that had been attempting to outflank them and raced over, his wings nearly taking Stan's head off. The visor in the suit made it hard to look sideways so Stan had to turn his whole body to see where Saturn was heading in such a hurry. When he finally managed to get a clear view, his elation turned to utter dismay. There now streamed from the surface of Pluto a huge army of foot soldiers. He had no idea how many but the column seemed several miles wide and already several hundred miles long. There must have been hundreds of thousands – no, millions of ghost warriors from all ages of man since the dawn of Time, now scrambling from their underworld realm to meet them.

The great Dragon, Jupiter, was suddenly at their side. 'Enough of this!' he roared, 'I am not putting to fire any more of the souls from the Realm of the Dead, they are not our enemy, it's time we paid my brother a visit!'

Even Mars looked doubtful. 'How do you propose to get down to Hades? We'll have to fight through them first.'

'Fire dome,' replied Jupiter, brusquely, 'but we'll have to be quick. Hades will see us coming and try and escape.' He may even try to harm the girl.' Jupiter glanced at Stan and saw the look on the boy's face. 'Though he may regret that.'

By now Saturn, Neptune, Mercury and Venus had fought their way over. The first wave of attack was in complete disarray and the souls of the dead were fleeing. They had a couple of minutes before the new horde was upon them.

'We're going to combine our fires to make a sphere,' said Mars as they came up.

'Well, I hope it works,' said Mercury, 'I'm parched, nearly out of fire.'

'I, too,' gasped Saturn.

'Not me!' said Mars, skipping from side to side, 'Still plenty in the tank!' But Stan, who still sat astride the Dragon, could feel his flanks heave as he drew breath.

'Better not delay, then,' and Jupiter's gold flame was joined by Saturn's swirling jet of bronze, Neptune's blue ice and then the rest: silver, purple and deep red. The heat was immense and Stan could feel

it even through his protective armour. Slowly the flames seemed to combine to produce a latticework of fire, like a giant Aura, all around them and the Dragons' wings now began to beat in time with one another. The wind from the wings swirled about Stan and the ball of flame revolved, like a small planet. Stan looked through the lattice and saw the first creatures of Hades' larger army rush the Fire Dome and veer away, or burst into flames. As the dome's revolutions increased, the path it created through the stream of the horde became wider and the Dragons picked up speed towards Pluto.

Down and down they went to the dark, icy planet, passing its moons as a huge ravine opened up before them and Stan saw the remains of a giant castle made of sharp ice and dark rock. He kept his sword unsheathed but there seemed little use for it as the dome was deflecting their attackers with ease, bodies of the dead were smashed against it or flung back into open Space. There was already a floating circular sea of dry bones about Pluto, like its own macabre ring of Saturn.

Down they went towards the wrecked castle and saw a great hall at its centre and an orange glow of fires deep below the frozen and dead surface of the planet. The Realm of the Dead.

Without warning, a jet of black, sooty fire shot out to the dome, but it simply bounced off the revolving surface as they smashed through the already broken roof of the great hall, each Dragon extinguishing their fire as the dome collapsed and seven very angry Dragons charged at a terrified-looking black Dragon whom Stan assumed was Hades.

Mars was in the lead with Stan still on his back, and he pinned the much smaller black Dragon by his wings to the floor.

For a moment it seemed as if Mars would rip out Hades' throat. His huge jaws opened and his head flicked back as he prepared to lunge.

'Wait!' Jupiter shuffled forward, shook himself and clicked a few neck joints. 'I'm getting too old for this nonsense,' he muttered as much to himself as anyone. 'Mars, my dear boy, perhaps you would be so good as to not bite your uncle's head off.' Mars relaxed but still kept two huge claws pinning Hades' wing membrane to the stone floor. 'And brother, much as I'd like to think up some awful punishment for all the trouble you have caused, any ideas of Dragon revenge will have to wait. First of all, call off your army.'

'Consider it done,' squeaked the small black

Dragon. 'Cerby, open the Styx portal.' The three-headed hound launched itself into the air. Jupiter nodded, like a satisfied headmaster.

'Secondly, and more importantly, where is the girl?'

Stan pushed his visor up and looked around.

'Stan, Stan, *Stan!*' Poppy, looking a little paler than normal, her nightie a bit grubby but otherwise the same as usual came rushing out of the shadows. Stan slid off the back of Mars.

Eight Dragons now witnessed the most awkward hug in the universe since the dawn of time.*

'Oh, hello Poppy,' Stan mumbled. If she kissed him there was a very good chance he might chop her head off with the sword. He knew it was very wrong but this was even more embarrassing than when his mum kissed him in front of the whole school when he won the Year 5 prize for Best Effort in Science.

'Stan, Stan. Stan!'

Stan glanced at the assembled Dragons who were all looking down at the two small Humans in interested silence.

'Stan ... Stan ... *STAN?*'

---

* It was more awkward than the hug Athena gave Medusa at the Gorgon office Christmas party of 15,000 BC, or the Cyclops who tried to hug Jason of the Argonauts but, having no depth vision, fell out of a window instead.

'Yes, *what?*'

'Can we go home now?'

He opened his mouth to say something reassuring, like his dad would do, but before he could answer Hades' cold, dark voice cut across the echoing room.

'Oh, I'm afraid it's much too late for that.'

CHAPTER XIV

Titans were giants of incredible strength
who ruled in the Golden Age.
Huge deposits of the ultra tough metal, titanium,
are found on the Moon.

❄

MARS RELUCTANTLY RELEASED HADES, who slithered off and crouched in a corner under the menacing glare of his family. A smaller, equally uncomfortable family group, consisting of Stan and Poppy, stood to one side. Hades had the sickly grin on his face of one who has lost the battle but still hopes to win the war.

'My army was just a delaying tactic,' he spat out clouds of black smoke, like a bad exhaust on a lorry, 'your real enemy is already here, on the other side of our system.'

'How?' Saturn's circular markings swirled in anger. Mars fumed.

'Oh, Father dear, the minute it left Earth's pro-

tective cradle, the Particle of Light called them.'

The Dragons turned to stare at Poppy, who smiled shyly back at them all. Stan noticed that none of them approached: they knew the Particle of Light and feared its power.

'The Titans mass on the far side of the Sun, as we speak. The battleground – your doom – will be the field of Phoebus.'

'We should have got rid of that thing last time round,' was Mars' opinion.

'We looked, but no one found it,' said Mercury.

'It remained hidden from us, until it was needed.' Venus interrupted. 'Do you not see? We can use it to finish the Titans once and for all. If we get it into the Sun before they can stop us, the solar flare when we re-unite the Particle of Light with its Mother Star will destroy them. Unlike us, they cannot withstand fire.'

'No! The Titans are too strong, even for you,' sneered Hades. 'Last time they were young, not full grown. They have spent their time brooding in Deep Space, feeding on Dark Matter, they are pure cosmic power and they will destroy you and then the Particle before you get anywhere near the Sun. You are fools if you think differently.'

And Stan was surprised to see doubt written

across the faces of the other Dragons. Could Hades be right? Stan had thought they had won, but now it seemed the real battle hadn't even started. He wondered if the Dragons were powerful enough to withstand the Titans, then wondered if he was. A few of them shuffled nervously but Jupiter just smiled a long slow Dragon grin. 'We have the Particle of Light and something else you haven't counted on, brother,' he said slowly, as if talking to an idiot.

'Oh yes, and what might that be ... *brother?*'

Jupiter smiled and pointed a claw at Stan and Poppy.

'We have heroes with us.'

'And they will die with you, too, then,' scoffed Hades.

'We shall see, we shall see,' said Jupiter, apparently unconcerned by Hades, although the others looked less sure. 'There are eight of us ... oh yes, you are coming too, Hades, and with that hound of yours. We fly to meet them now ... perhaps the time of the Titans has finally come and they will overthrow the Planet Dragons. We shall see.' And, once more, Jupiter seemed to shrug off his elderly kindliness and become a fearsome creature full of majesty. He spread his wings and roared. 'We fly to what might

191

be our last great battle!'

be right? Stan had thought they had won, but now it seemed the real battle hadn't even started. He wondered if the Dragons were powerful enough to

※

Stan watched a film once with his dad about Titans. He couldn't remember much about them apart from that they were huge, like giants of giants, and they had a fight with the gods. He was pretty sure the gods won that time but his suit was hot and sweaty and he began to feel nervous again – a feeling quickly replaced by annoyance when he looked sideways and saw Poppy riding Venus with a big smile on her face, as if all of this was the most normal thing in the world. She waved enthusiastically at him, and he shrugged and turned away. He knew he should be pleased she was safe, but she was still annoying. And this was his adventure. If she hadn't stolen his crystal none of this might have happened. Even worse than that, she'd been given a suit similar to the Febus Armour – but in silver and edged with rubies. It hadn't been made by Wayland, but by one of his apprentices. It still looked pretty cool.

They were streaking across the solar system at several times light speed, so fast that the planets they did pass were a blur, as their fire corridors somehow combined to make a wormhole through which they raced, liked a giant flume, across the heavens.

They had travelled like this for hours and the Sun was slowly expanding before them. Stan had read somewhere that it took the light eleven hours to go from the Sun to the end of the Solar System: he realised that this must be draining the Dragons' power, and all this after the battle with the forces of Hades. They would arrive exhausted and would then have to fight the strongest beings ever created.

He'd felt proud when Jupiter said he had the blood of heroes, but right now he would have settled for being a normal boy in Year 7.

He looked over at Poppy again ... they should have dropped her off at Earth and given him the Particle —

BANG!

It felt like a massive explosion, sending him sideways. He'd been travelling in Mercury's slipstream,

pulled along in the wake of the fastest Dragon's Aura; using some, but not all of his own power from the suit. The Febus Armour had been made for a sun god and as he'd got closer to the Sun, he'd felt its energy increase. He was glad because the force of the impact was tremendous, like being hit by a giant fist out of nowhere.

As if on cue – and out of nowhere – a giant fist appeared again. This was one occasion Stan wasn't pleased about being right the first time.

This time it bludgeoned both Saturn and Neptune, spinning them sideways and into the path of an oncoming meteorite, which smashed into hundreds of smaller meteorites when Jupiter's tail swiped it aside.

More meteorites came, coming fast from all directions. 'They're throwing big rocks at us!' shouted Mercury.

'Cheats!' Saturn looked thoroughly indignant. 'I can't even see the blighters.'

'Of course you can't, they're hiding in Dark Matter,' Jupiter explained.

Stan squinted and could just about make out a huge black shadow, more like a sort of hole in the canopy of stars all around. It was the size of a skyscraper, roughly the shape of a man and it was

bounding towards them. 'Look out!' he cried. Mars banked and roared out a tumbling wave of fire. The flames hit the shape and it became visible: a colossal, heavily muscled giant briefly swathed in Mars' red flames that gave it shape and made the Titan even more terrifying.

The burning Titan roared, whether in pain or anger it was hard to say. This time the fist that came towards them was swathed in a billowing furnace and Mars had to swerve sharply to avoid it, nearly hitting Stan in the process. As the monstrous arm flashed by, Stan swung his sword and was pleased to feel the blade bite, going through flesh and bone, neatly chopping off the Titan's middle finger. A sort of sickly yellow blood spurted from the wound, which immediately fizzled away into cold space. They were getting very close to the Sun now. Stan whooped – he'd actually wounded a Titan! But his arm had gone numb: the impact had run up the sword and vibrated through his whole body. It was like cutting through solid granite.

The Titan roared again and went for a sideswipe. This time he connected, although luckily the fire was out, otherwise Stan would have been fried. Both Stan, with his arm and shoulder in numb agony, and Mars, went careering across open space.

'Well *done*, my boy!' said Mars, banking out of his chaotic tumble, spitting out some broken teeth and grinning. 'I've never seen anyone able to do that, took his whole finger off in one swipe. That was Crios, he's the most bad-tempered of the lot. You've made a powerful enemy there! Splendid, I love enemies!'

Stan nodded mutely, he wasn't sure if he could swing the sword again, his sword arm still felt completely dead.

Meteorites and assorted space rubble was raining down on them from all sides now. Dodging it was hard enough but Stan looked this way and that, trying to see Poppy and work out how many Titans there might be. He climbed back onto Mars' shoulders and prepared for battle. 'You must get the girl away!' he heard Jupiter shout to Venus.

'But ...' Venus obviously felt she was needed in battle, but Jupiter looked serious.

'No, I've read the slow stars deep in the Spiral Arm Nebular, daughter ... you can't possibly imagine how important this one is.'

Venus hesitated for a second, then bowed very briefly, turned with Poppy safely in her Aura and headed towards a large meteorite just out of the danger zone. As Stan readied himself for battle

again, he glanced over and watched Venus land in a shadowed alcove, like a cave. She'll be safe, he thought with relief and with surprise that protecting her had started to come so naturally without his parents around.

Not that it would make any difference where she was if they lost the battle to come: if that happened, Stan had a bad feeling that no one, anywhere, would be truly safe ever again.

Mercury shot over. He looked tired and his liquid silver hide seemed duller than usual and less mobile. 'Well done Stan, I knew you were special, first time I clapped eyes on you ... you know, what you did there reminds me of the time Hercules fought the Hydra – not that I had anything against that particular monster ... whoaah ...' he paused as they all ducked a well-aimed meteor. 'Phew ... where was I? Hydra – gentlest creature in mythology, in fact, mostly vegetarian, brilliant babysitters, but old Hercie thought it would be good for his image, all those heads with their dripping jaws being chopped off and growing back ...'

'Mercury ... not to be rude, but we're a bit — '

'OOOOH, WATCH OUT!' A huge lump of ice suddenly appeared out of nowhere, flung at great speed. Mercury shoved Stan out of the way as the

ice boulder came so close he felt pressure waves push him back.

That was the problem, Stan realised – fighting in a vacuum made it hard to stay in one place and get your balance. Even the small debris from broken rocks being hurled bounced off his armour and pushed him about. The Dragons had their wings to hold them steady, Stan was having to learn fast to use the suit's energy in small bursts.

As he came out of a tumble, there was a strange noise – it reminded Stan of an airliner coming in to land. He, Mercury, and Mars turned to watch, frozen to the spot as the noise hurtled towards them, Stan frantically trying to work out what it was and whether it was a threat. Then in a flash of hyperdrive, Jupiter burst onto the battlefield – a golden streak out of nowhere, he launched himself at the dark shape that was hurling the lumps of rock and ice.

As Jupiter's huge body crashed into the near-invisible Titan, the giant chose to reveal itself.

Stan felt his mouth drop open in shock and awe as he tried to take in the sheer size of the creature Jupiter was fighting. One glance really didn't seem enough, it needed time to get the scale of the monster from his eyes into his brain. Next to it, the

largest Dragon in the Solar System looked like a small lizard.

The Titan's head was almost Human, though it was covered in pits and gouges, like the surface of the Moon, as if its face in deep space had been struck thousands of times, making huge holes pitted by meteorites and space debris. Bits of its mostly naked body had grown huge patches of permafrost, which had solidified into stone. The giant was made more of rock than flesh, and it roared in rage and pain as it tried to squeeze the life out of Jupiter, who was pouring fire into its face.

'That's Atlas!' Mars looked over his shoulder. 'He's the strongest of them all!' Behind Atlas, the rest of the Titans now detached themselves from the blackness all around, leaving the shelter of the Dark Matter to step forward into the blazing light of the fast-approaching Sun.

Stan did a rough count and saw there were over a hundred. Not all as large as their leader, some more creature than humanoid giant: with flailing tentacles, fish heads, foreheads full of eyes, quite a few were little more than lumps of rock and ice with rudimentary hands and arms – but they all had the same hugeness. Stan took a deep breath and tried to calm himself without much luck: Hades had been

right, the Dragons really didn't stand a chance.

Predictably, Mars didn't quite see it that way. 'Finally someone worth fighting!' he cried, 'Let's go, Stan, my boy, this will be ... *fun!*' With that he made straight for a Titan wielding a huge rusting sword of bronze and iron, ducking under a swipe that missed his wing membranes by a hand's width. Stan had no time to duck, all he could do to avoid losing his head was raise his still numb sword arm as the Titan's ancient blade came down.

Their blades met just ... *so.*

Stan's sword had been forged by the greatest smithy in history, and cared for over the centuries. Its shaft, whose metal was mined from a distant star, was tougher than diamond. The Titan's blade was huge, but crudely made for size and weight, not skill. It was more a club than a cutter. It had also been out in deep space for over ten thousand years and had suffered the extremes of heat and cold, like its master.

As the blades crashed together there was a blinding cascade of sparks and a noise like a boulder splitting in two.

The Titan's sword had shattered, sending needle sharp slivers of metal the size of splintered oaks in all directions. At least six of the Titans staggered

back roaring in pain and rage, spears of the fragmented sword embedding themselves in torsos, arms, legs, and in one of the Titans' eyes. It staggered back, blindly flailing an ice club that scattered the front rank.

Into the gap Mercury, Neptune and Saturn flew, spewing their fire, creating temporary mayhem in the other ranks.

'You did it!' shouted Mars over his shoulder, looking genuinely surprised and incredibly impressed. 'We've opened up their defences, thanks to you!'

We could do this, Stan thought. Life was very strange, these days. Only a week ago he was worried about what to do with the rest of the summer, wondering if they would get time to visit the seaside or Center Parks. Now he felt like he was in a film.

Except this was very real and so was the danger.

Both Mars and he had taken their eye off the Titan with the broken sword to revel in the chaos Stan had caused. This was a mistake.

The Titan may have been big, but he was also fast. He threw away his useless weapon and in the same movement made a grab for Mars, his colossal fingers easily encircling the red Dragon's body. Stan

kicked himself away and used his suit's power to gain height over the battle.

Mars gasped in pain as the Titan brought him close to his huge mouth, with its broken teeth the size of jutting boulders and purple lips that dripped saliva. Mars looked alarmed for a moment, then very angry. Stan readied himself to turn to try to do something to save him being eaten; in the end, though, he needn't have bothered. Mars' long neck snaked back like a whip and then shot forward. All the force of his very hard skull (whose bone was almost three feet thick in places and very knobbly) hit the surprised Titan square between the eyes.

The giant let out a groan that made Stan's armour vibrate and fell backwards, out cold.

'Ha!' shouted Mars, looking a bit dazed himself, it had to be said. 'Who's next?'

Stan banked and raced back down to the centre of the fight, feeling the suit become more responsive the more he got used to it. His arm had got back some of its feeling and the suit was humming with solar energy. He was aiming at the lead Titan who was grappling with Jupiter, so he didn't notice an arm reach out to grab him. Luckily Neptune did and Stan was amazed to see blue fire, a liquid jet of nitrogen, streak across the blackness and encase

the top half of the Titan in ice.

The Titan, one head a giant cockerel, and the other a drooling old man, cried out in pain and fell away. Neptune nodded at Stan who gave a 'thumbs up' sign. Out of the corner of his eye, he could see Jupiter was losing his battle. If Jupiter fell, the Dragons would be finished. Stan spurred the suit forward, making it go faster than he'd ever dared, aiming a blow at the back of Atlas' head. His sword connected but it did little more than gash the back of the Titan's neck. However, it was enough to make Atlas relax his grip on Jupiter who saw his chance and squeezed out of his attacker's grasp.

Mercury was using his speed to zip between the giants and Saturn sent out well-timed bursts of fire as their heads turned to follow the messenger of the gods.

Had they been a bit younger, had they been less exhausted from their race to get to the Sun and had there been just a few less Titans, they might have turned the battle in their favour at this point.

But the sheer size and the numbers of Titans began to tell. At the start of the battle, they had continued to head towards the Sun, but now an impenetrable wall of Titans had formed between them and their goal. On all fronts they seemed to be

losing the fight. Stan looked over and saw Mars weaving between the giants. He was still laughing through his bloodied mouth but Stan noticed scales had been torn from his flanks and he was bleeding heavily; Mercury was a dull lead colour, and his fire barely more than a thin jet; As for Saturn, his wings had shredded and he was struggling to hold off a smaller Titan with concentrated bursts of fire. Even the great Dragon, Jupiter, looked exhausted.

Throughout all this, Hades and his dog Cerberus had stood to one side. Hades was now beginning to look triumphant – he must have been glad he was forced to come, victory was almost his and he was there to witness his moment in time.

The end of the old gods was almost at hand – a forgotten era, briefly resurrected by a seemingly insignificant Human boy and an equally seemingly insignificant crystal. This would soon be the end, the last of the Planet Dragons sent back to myth.

But Hades, and perhaps everyone else, had quite forgotten about one small girl.

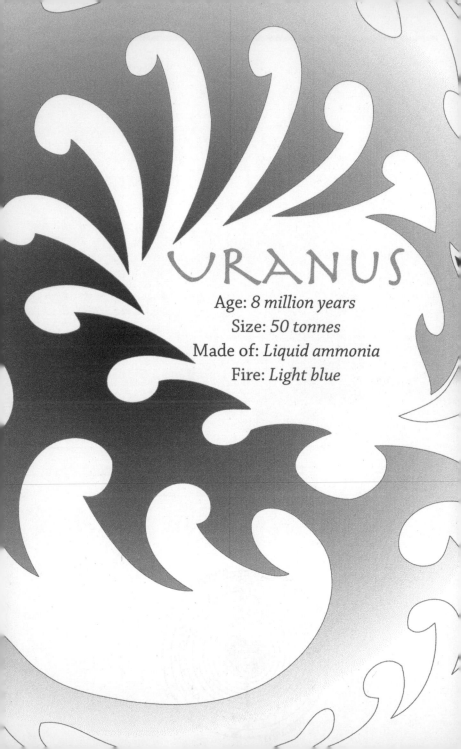

URANUS

Age: *8 million years*
Size: *50 tonnes*
Made of: *Liquid ammonia*
Fire: *Light blue*

DEUS EX MACHINA

✲

POPPY, WITH HER BEADY-BRIGHT EYES, spied a gap in the jets of flame criss-crossing frozen space. She was also the only one who spotted the bright plume of a comet that flew like a burning arrow towards the Sun. She hadn't really understood everything that Stan had explained a bit grumpily to her, except that granny's crystal in her pocket was special because it was part of the Sun and they had to put it back where it belonged. Being told to put things back had been a big part of her life up until now. And that was all she needed to know.

She wasn't very good yet at guiding her suit, but she knew if she went tiptoes, she would go forward ... very fast indeed ...

'Wait!' Venus cried out as Poppy shot from the Dragon's protective Aura, but it was too late, Poppy was away and streaking towards her goal.

Venus was not the only person who noticed her peel off. Just to her left, Poppy saw the great big dog, Cerberus; she saw two of its three heads whip around and its huge paws extend as it left Hades' side and raced towards her in great galloping strides that ate up the distance until she could see, with fright, she wasn't going to make it – the nasty dog was going to get her first. Poppy had no idea what it would do, probably bite her and shake her in its giant jaws until she was all floppy – like Boris when he'd stolen her teddy in the garden. But she knew in her small heart she still had to get the Particle of Light onto the comet as it curled towards the flaming Sun and then Stan would say it was all OK and they would be best friends again.

And they would go home.

She pointed her feet even more, like in ballet, and felt a jolt of speed. In fact, now she was pulling away from the black dog and she thought would make it, but just then her attention was caught by the great dog's master, Hades, whose black features turned to see where Cerberus was going. The dark Dragon's jaws opened wide.

Poppy was terrified and her feet instinctively started to run, as if to pedal the air in panic, which only slowed her down. She realised her mistake too

208

late, Cerberus would be snapping at her any second. She felt tears of frustration well up, she had spoiled everything again ... Stan would be really cross ... but then she had an idea.

Her arm went back.

The Particle of Light arced away from her hands, all the force of her small shoulder going into the throw.

'Fetch!' she shouted, as if they were playing with Boris in the garden.

Cerberus turned and one of its heads grabbed at the Particle of Light on instinct alone. Whatever power was in the small stone was enough to cause the hound's fur to light up and its skeleton was suddenly visible like in a huge x-ray. He howled as the force of the blast threw him into the path of the comet flare and disappeared.

Then there was a black heat, like burning coal all around her.

But Poppy felt nothing.

Apart from a lightness, a sort of relief, like she had been worried about something and now it didn't matter. And suddenly the suit didn't seem all big and uncomfortable, it felt fine, and she was still moving, out of the black fire that came from Hades and into the light – a white light, brighter even than

the Sun. And little Poppy was laughing because she knew she'd done it and everyone would say 'clever girl!' and Stan would hold her hand. Even.

All the way home.

She was going home.

❄

Stan held onto Poppy as hard as he could: when Mercury came over he wouldn't let go. She could have been just sleeping ... except.

She wasn't.

But Stan just wouldn't let himself believe she was dead.

The battle was over, there had been a flash of white and the comet had raced away. The Titans, sensing something, had lowered their weapons and turned, some had made it to the Dark Matter, some had been swept away in the fire when the comet hit the Sun. The battle had been won but Stan wasn't watching: he'd seen a black plume of polluted fire from Pluto and Poppy ... her small body had just disappeared in it.

And for the first time Stan knew what it felt like to care more about someone other than himself. Really care. And really be sorry.

And it wasn't just that Poppy was his sister. What she had done had been the bravest thing he had ever seen. But she was his sister and instead of being proud, as he should have been, because she had been with Hades and survived and kept the Particle of Light safe, he'd just been grumpy ... and when she was cheerful because he was there, he'd always been nasty, because her in a good mood somehow made him in a bad mood.

So, Stan cried, and what's more, he didn't care who could see.

'I must be the worst brother in the world.' Stan said, not looking at Mercury.

'In the Universe, in fact. There's nothing like expanding your world view to put what a little twit you are into context.'

Stan looked up to see a very elderly Dragon, swathed in rock and ice, who made Saturn and Jupiter look positively youthful.

'Great Granddad!' breathed Mercury. 'Cripes!'

'Yes, well, I woke up and everyone had gone, so I guessed something very important must be happening. Didn't want to miss history or anything.'

Stan looked over vaguely at the very old Dragon. Then he looked back at Poppy, tears running down his face.

'What seems to be the problem here, young man?'

'She's dead,' Stan's voice cracked.

'Oh, I doubt that very much.'

'Ah, Hades,' the father of all Dragons – known to some as Sidus, others Caelus, and, to legions of delighted children, Uranus – now looked very angry. 'You have been causing trouble again.'

'Grandfather ...' began the small, black Dragon flanked by Mars and Venus, 'I ...'

'None of your excuses, I think. You were given a job you don't much like – I don't blame you for wanting to get away from that miserable dark planet with all those dead people and that chilly castle. But you've done this,' he pointed an ancient claw at Poppy's lifeless body. 'What do you propose to do about it?'

Hades face went blank for a few moments. 'Yes, she is in the Realm of the Dead, already, I can see her. She is mine.'

'Oh no she's not,' Uranus snapped, 'you can start by giving her back, is that clear?'

Hades gave a sickly smile. 'But as you say, Grandfather dear, I have Dominion over the Dead. I rule there, you cannot make me give her up! She is mine and she will remain there until the Arch of Time is broken.'

Stan, through his grief, heard what Hades was saying. He blinked.

He suddenly realised what he had come out to Space for: it wasn't about the Particle – Poppy had shown she had more control over this than he did; it wasn't about the adventure; it wasn't even for his skill with the sword ... no, he had gone out there for a reason, one reason only, his job had been clear: he was there to bring Poppy back home.

Hades was too busy looking triumphant to notice Stan surge forward, draw his sword in one graceful movement and bring the razor sharp edge to within a millimetre of the Dragon's exposed neck.

'Give. My. Sister. Back.' Stan said very quietly. Hades would have gulped, but the sword was so close any movement risked cutting his own throat. Dragons very rarely have to think about their own death, but Hades saw that his was seconds away.

'Yes, of course, right away,' he managed in a terrified whisper.

'Boy.'

Stan was still glaring at Hades.

'You boy!' the voice said louder, but not unkindly.

Stan turned to see Uranus grinning at him. 'Well, you have just defeated your first Dragon, well done, no doubt they'll start naming pubs after you! We

will see to it that Hades will return your sister, after you have been so, ah, persuasive. My son, Saturn, controls time, he will now send you both back to your own dimension. Of course, you'll have to go back to your own time-space-continuum thingy slightly before all this nonsense started. And you won't remember a thing, I'm sorry to say.'

'Nothing at all?' asked Stan.

'No, technically none of this will have happened. You'll be your old self.'

'Oh,' said Stan. His old self might have minded but now he was just glad to get Poppy back safe and sound.

Uranus turned to Saturn. 'My son, would you mind ... ? We've got a lot of clearing up to do and I'd like to get started and go home for rest.'

'Yes,' said Saturn, 'of course. Although ...'

'Although what?'

'I've been looking at the stars again.'

'What now?' Uranus scowled.

'There is a threat coming, far greater than the one we have just faced ... Atlas and some of the stronger Titans escaped the blast: they will call our Nemesis: the Deep Space Dragons.' He looked serious. 'I believe the Second Age of Heroes is once more upon us.'

'Well in that case, Stan,' Uranus, Father of Dragons patted a huge claw fondly on Stan's armoured shoulder, 'farewell for now, but I expect we'll be seeing you and your sister soon: no doubt we will need your sister's quick thinking and that sword of yours in the near future!'

EXODE

(the before ... but after)

Stan Pollux, Year 7 pupil and demigod (although he didn't know it), woke up on the first day of the summer holidays and looked out the window.

It was bright and sunny and he was keen to get out.

Stan heard his sister, Poppy, in the garden. She was singing as she went to the shed and Stan vaguely remembered promising to play with her. He hadn't said exactly when, so he felt fine about going out for a ride first. He'd be back for lunch and his mum would probably make him stay at home afterwards anyway.

Stan grabbed a faded t-shirt and his lucky Ben Ten pants from the day before – wincing as he squeezed them on – and pulled on his jeans. He was fiddling with the laces on his trainers by the front door, trying to get the knot untangled, when his mum walked past with the post. 'Poppy said to tell you she's making you a delicious meal in the shed.' she said, flicking through the junk mail.

'Hmmyurr,' mumbled Stan who was using the pull-as-hard-as-you-can-on-one-end of the laces technique with the left trainer. It wasn't especially successful, but he managed to force the trainer on anyway and set off down the garden.

'Stan: breakfast!' his mother called after him, giving up with the post and throwing the lot in the magazine recycling basket. Stan sighed under his breath, circled back and picked up an apple from the fruit bowl in the kitchen. As he did so, something caught his eye. On top of the pile of local supermarket adverts, pizza delivery deals and things about the millions of pounds in prizes they had not really already won, was a flyer for the DIY shop he went to sometimes with his dad on Saturday mornings. **Prices out of this world!!** and a picture of the planet Saturn with its rings. When Stan looked at it he got a funny feeling right in the pit of his stomach. He was interested in Space and planets but this wasn't excitement, it was more like a kind of *trepidation* – a word he'd recently learned at school – it meant excitement and fear at the same time.

When his dad went away, the last thing he always said to Stan was, 'Remember, you're in charge, so look after the girls.' Stan always thought that was a joke but something now made him think of it.

'Where are you going in such a hurry, anyway?' Mum asked.

'I'm off for a bike ride. On my own.'

'Oh,' said his mother, frowning slightly. 'I think Poppy's expecting you to play with her.'

'But ...' it had been on the tip of his tongue to say no, or complain. But today was different. He didn't know why but everything felt a bit different – you know, the way it sometimes does.

Stan went into the garden to find his sister. 'Let's go for a bike ride,' he said when he found her. 'It'll stop you going in my room, when I'm out.' Poppy grinned and dashed off at super light speed.

Ten minutes later they were heading into the village. His sister's tiny bicycle was too slow and she kept on stopping to get off and push at the hilly bits. 'When I start proper school, I'm going to be in the big classroom next to the playground and I'll have a packed lunch every day. And I'll see you at playtimes.' She smiled up at her brother, who shrugged. They were coming around the last corner. 'Look, there's that nasty boy with his friends.'

Stan glanced up from his handlebars and felt his heart sink. Guy Murphy was already smiling unpleasantly, which meant he had seen them and there was no way Stan would be able to turn his bike around now and cycle the other way.

'Stammering Stan, and his annoying little sister. Seriously, is she the only friend you've got?'

'You be quiet!' shouted Poppy, but ruined the effect by missing a pedal and nearly falling off.

'Well, I wonder who's going in the bin today?' said Guy moving towards Poppy.

Up until he said that, Stan was about to cycle past, but the threat made him stop. He looked at Guy and suddenly thought to himself, *I've had enough of this*. Poppy stopped too and watched her brother get slowly off his bike and walk towards the bully. Stan was a lot bigger than Guy and this was made more obvious when he got really close.

'What are you going to do, dribble on me?' Guy looked at his friends for support, but they'd noticed a look in Stan's eye they hadn't seen before and a new confidence in the way he crowded Guy, and all of them kept quiet today. Stan stepped forward a pace, forcing Guy to move back, then forward again. 'Push off Pollux.' He tried to shove Stan, but he was off-balance and the shove made him slip, his arms suddenly windmilling as solid ground turned into a ditch and he fell backwards.

Stan's calm expression did not change as he jumped down into the ditch after Guy. Placing his legs either side of his body he grabbed him by the front of his shirt and pulled him close. Guy closed his eyes and let out a small whimper. Stan took a deep breath and glared at Guy as everyone went very still. And waited. Was he going to hit Guy?

'Supercalifragilisticexpialidocious,' said Stan, then he turned, and winked at the watching children who had burst out laughing, more with nerves as the tension was released.

Poppy didn't really understand fighting or what had actually gone on, except the boy called Guy had said he was sorry after that and he even said it to Poppy when Stan told him to.

As they cycled home, she smiled up at him, but all squinty because the sun was in her eyes.

Stan looked a bit grumpy at first but she knew he was just pretending because, slowly, something like another sun was coming out in Poppy's world ...

He smiled back.

(The End)